FRIENDS WE HAVEN'T MET

Abby Chicken,
Is that really
your last name?

Ksc Hatch

First published in 2016 by Sonam Press via www.lulu.com
ISBN 978-1-365-02263-0

Fonts:
Title: Amatic SC, Body text: Cochin, Quote: Jellyka Delicious Cake

This is a work of fiction. Names, characters, businesses, places, events
and incidents are either the products of the author's imagination or used in a
fictitious manner. Any resemblance to actual persons, living or dead, or actual
events is purely coincidental except when it isn't because they always say 'write
what you know' and so most characters in books are probably inspired by
people the author knows, in as much as anyone can 'know' another person.

This book is sold subject to the condition that it be lent, shared, spread
around, talked about in book clubs, amongst friends, family & lovers and
enjoyed by as many people as possible. If you find that you're not enjoying it,
the author suggests you stop and read something else, because life is too brief
to spend it reading things you don't value. Whether you enjoy this book or not,
she recommends the works of A.M Homes, Kate Atkinson, Christopher Moore,
Joanne Harris, Terry Pratchett, Kurt Vonnegut and Neil Gaiman.

To the neutrals.

ACKNOWLEDGMENTS

I could have put this at the back of the book, which is where acknowledgements often go, but I wanted it at the start because this book wouldn't even exist without the help of a multitude of people.

It's important to me that you know this book is not the work of one individual, but a big and beautiful example of interconnectedness. If we really get into it, there are the people who grew the trees and chopped the wood and pulped the paper. The people who ran the machine that printed the text and bound the whole thing. The people who helped it through the post so it would eventually get to you. I am grateful to them and appreciate the multitude of unseen ways in which we are helped every day by people we will never meet.

But these acknowledgements are chiefly for the people whose efforts have been more visible to me. Without their support, this book wouldn't be the real, actual thing you are currently holding. I hope I have included everyone—any missed names are an unfortunate and unintended oversight on my part.

This was a crowd-funded project. Every individual contribution accumulated in enough funds to cover the costs of editing, printing and distribution. In the original campaign perks, I offered to list the names of the Silver and Gold patrons in these acknowledgements. Because the people who backed at the Silver and Gold levels happen to be my wife and my parents (They're getting special thanks, regardless.) I would like to use this space to thank every backer by name because they're all Awesome and because I can!

So thank you to:

The Digital Patrons: Annie, Clara, Emily, Jill, Leila, Paul, Peta, Sarah, and Val.

The Paper Patrons: Angela, Ariela, Cielia, Georgie, Guy, Jackie, Jamie, Jeremy, Jessica, Kim, Lee, Rob, Sarah, Starr, Sue, Tina and Zabine.

The Aluminium Patrons: Athea, Alexis, Anton, Bethany, Caroline, Claude, James, Susan, Kendra, Mitch, Natalie, Pennie, Rachel, Sarah, Sierra, Tova, Tylea and Whitney.

The Copper Patrons: Abby, Anne-Francoise, Annette, Bonnie, Chris, Cindy, Ewa, Rita, Janet, John, Juanita, Julie, K, Keiko, Kit, Kris, Linda, Lyn, Mammen, Martin, Monica, Nick, Nicole, Patti, Ross and Silas.

The Bronze Patrons: Arantza & Stephan and Michele

Thank you to Tylea Richard for making time to answer my questions about running a crowdfunding campaign. Her blog and underwear are fantastic and her help prior to the campaign launch did so much to prepare me.

Thank you to all the people who helped promote the campaign through social media, but notably: Chris Byers, Lyn Langille, Janet Harrison, Athea Merredyth, Angyl Bender and my brother, Nick Hatch. Special shout out to Bif Naked, Annie

Sprinkle, Christopher Moore, Naheed Nenshi and Joanne Harris for sharing the campaign through their Twitter and Facebook accounts, and to Chris Brecheen and Angela Hefner for promoting the campaign through their blogs. And thank you, Katie Herzig, for giving me permission to use the song Best Day of Your Life in a promotional campaign video—if you go to my website and click on the YouTube icon at the top of the page you can watch it!

Thank you to the creators of National Novel Writing Month! I wrote the first draft of the manuscript during NaNoWriMo 2012, just a few weeks after learning that it existed. The community support and tools made writing 50,000 words in one month much easier than I could have imaged.

I'd also like to thank my editor, Eric Emily Satchwill, for their feedback, guidance and expertise. Though they weren't able to see the project to the final proofing stage due to unforeseeable circumstances, they did a fantastic job reviewing the structure, plot and narrative/character consistency. I trust that you will enjoy this book all the more for their part in it.

Super-duper huge thank you to Nicole Byers for helping promote the campaign, finding the venue for the book launch *and* coming through to do the final proofing of the manuscript.

I would like to thank my parents for their unwavering support in everything I do, all the time. Shannon and Julian are two of my biggest fans. They have always encouraged my writing, my artistic endeavours and my insatiable curiosity, without which I wouldn't have such a passion for learning and teaching myself All the Things.

And finally, I want to thank the love of my life, my unicorn, best friend and wife: Gretchen Wagner. She made it possible for me to go to work every day, all day, as a writer. I do not think I can ever adequately express my gratitude, appreciation and wonderment for the support she has given me with this project— and in all things. I adore you, I appreciate you, I love you.

Thank you.

Be kind, for most of us are fighting a hard battle

- Unknown

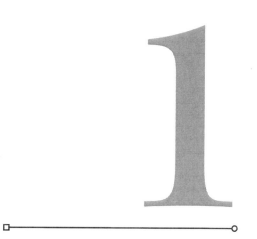

The trilling of a ringing phone fills a tiny apartment, disturbing the neighbour who has just gotten her small child off to sleep. She counts the rings through the too-thin walls, cringing with each one as she looks towards the closed bedroom door. It's nearly eleven at night. Who would ring at that time?

She hardly knows her neighbour. He's a young white man, younger than her but not by much. He has the gangly look of a web developer or Internet geek, pale beyond words with flushed pink cheeks and fair hair the colour of sun-drenched wheat with a hint of strawberries. The sort who never tans because burning happens so fast.

She doesn't know what he does, although he leaves the apartment often and is usually gone for long periods of time. She knows the movements of most of her neighbours because she doesn't have anywhere to go and nothing to distract her during the day. It's just her and the child—too young to be much company but old enough to be strong-willed and defiant.

It's all too clichéd in her world. He'd gone out to meet some buddies at the pub. He'd be back later, he said. He'd not made eye contact when he'd said it, but not out of shame. He'd been callous, flippant. Standing suddenly to pull on his jacket, as if his 'friends' had telepathically invited him. Or, more likely, as if he suddenly realised he had a way out and he could take it.

That was three months ago. Three months of just her and the child. She leaves to get food, only the bare necessities of course, but otherwise she's in the apartment day and night, listening to the neighbours.

Eleven rings at eleven o'clock. The phone goes silent. Just the hum of the refrigerator now, the ticking of the clock on the wall. Not a sound from the baby in the bedroom off to her left. She realises she's been holding her breath and now she fills her lungs.

The ringing starts again. Her breath catches in her throat. One, two, three. Whoever it is really wants an answer. She tries to think about the last time she's heard a noise from the flat next door. Was it yesterday? Or the day before that?

Her ears twitch like a mouse, tuned finely to the needs of the child whether she likes it or not. A soft sound, like a questioning sigh. She squeezes her tired eyes shut as the ringing next door begins again and the baby wakes and fills his lungs to scream.

She moves quickly, opening the door and scooping him up before the banging from the apartment to the other side can start. They've complained six times already—threatening to take it up with the building management. Well, *he's* complained more than she has. He's a 'tough piece of work'. That's what her ex had said.

Ex? Is she thinking of him as that already? It has been three months, after all. She thinks of her parents, her father's harsh words and angry face. "No good will come of it!"

"If you go with this man you are no daughter of mine." Her father in the doorway of her childhood home, surprisingly calm in his declaration. At the time she didn't understand how any parent could wish not to have their own child. She hates that he was right.

In her arms, the child ceases crying almost instantly. He flops his head onto her narrow shoulder, his own arms relax at his sides. Next door, the ringing starts up again. That's the fourth try. She wonders if she should knock. He mightn't even be in. She can't imagine someone ignoring that loud, rattling ring four times.

The child snuffles, pushing his head into her neck. She strokes his hair, soft and dark like hers. As the phone begins ringing for the fifth time, she makes up her mind.

~ o ~

"That damn kid is crying again." He clenches his fist around his beer bottle, as though it were a can and he could crush it.

"He's a kid. They cry." Normally she wouldn't be so bold in her retort but he's distracted by his football, dozy from his beer. She knows he won't lumber from his seat unless he feels he must.

"Fuckin' thing wouldn't cry if he was mine." He says it to sound mean but his voice is distracted, his eyes following the tiny men on the big green field as they chase their ball.

She doesn't have much fight in her either and knows that this won't turn into one of their usual rows. She hates those but at least she knows if they did have a fight, it wouldn't wake up the baby next door.

She's so envious of their neighbour. Here she is, over thirty and no child of her own. She looks at the hefty figure of her boyfriend—she couldn't bear to call him her 'partner'—and cringes at the thought of them making a child together.

Every time she sees their soft-spoken neighbour she feels a pang. She's never spoken to them, their encounters have been few and far between. There was that time she was leaving the flat just as they were returning. Happy family. Father looking down at his son, stroking his hair and tickling under his chin.

Mother fishing around for keys, glancing up to look at the father of her child.

She'd never heard the neighbours fight. She'd not heard much from next door for a while now. Just the baby crying every so often. That beautiful brown baby. There was a report on the telly that said kids like him were the future. Mixed babies everywhere now that the social taboo of interracial marriage was history. She tries imagining herself with a mixed baby, wondering what sort of man the father would be if his ancestry was entirely different from her own. Maybe she needs an Asian guy. She knows they're supposed to expect their wives to be doting and submissive but she's good at that anyway. Well, maybe not the submissive bit. The doting bit is more for the sake of appeasement. She gives as good as she gets when tempers fly.

She doesn't think an Asian guy would watch the football or drink beer. She's pretty sure they don't drink. Or some of them don't. She'd have to get one of the ones who doesn't drink.

She can even make curry, so that's good. The smell of it permeates the halls sometimes, coming from next door. She makes hers using those jars you can get in Costcutter. Easy as anything. Just cook up the ingredients and dump on the sauce. Serve it with a package of instant rice. She doesn't make it a lot, though. He's picky. Odd given that curry and football seemed to go hand in hand.

"I don't want that foreign muck," he would snort. Once she pointed out that he had no qualms about drinking their beer. That was a rip-roaring row.

At least he doesn't hit her. Not like the last one. He's just loud. Loud is okay. Loud doesn't leave bruises. Loud doesn't need makeup or trips to the hospital under the guise of having 'fallen down the stairs'.

She yells back to create a wall, but it still makes her flinch sometimes. Makes her remember when she was just a kid and no amount of anger helped protect her.

~ o ~

The knocking is almost inaudible at first. Like a timid mouse. It's strangely different after the sharpness of the ringing.

The flat is nearly silent, the silence like a cave around him. He has no clock ticking, no whirring computer hard drive or buzzing entertainment system.

The knocking grows a bit louder now. He wonders if he should get it, if moving is actually an option or if his muscles have atrophied. He doesn't think they could in such a short period of time, but you never know. In fact, when he tries to remember, he's uncertain about how long it's been since he's moved. Maybe it's not been so short after all.

He is surprised to have so many thoughts suddenly flowing through his head. He's gotten used to not thinking anything. He wonders if that's what it's like to be a Buddhist, if you can just turn off your thoughts. He's not sure if that's how it works.

The noise is out of his mouth before he realises it's him who's made it. He thinks he was trying to say hello or some similar greeting, but it comes out as a hoarse gargle. His throat is sore and dry and as he lifts his head, he feels it throbbing.

His flat is dark, the only light coming from the very small slit under the door to the hall. He can see the shadow of the person knocking, blocking the light from coming in.

"Go away." His voice is cracked. It sounds like a dead thing, a broken thing. He swallows hard and squeezes his eyes shut against the pain in his head. Now that he's moving, even if its ever so slightly, his muscles begin to cry out.

"I...Is everything all right?" asks a woman through the door.

Is everything all right? He smiles. No. No, everything is not all right. No. A person does not lie down on a couch and not move if everything is all right. A person doesn't neglect their basic needs, eating, drinking, going to the loo, if everything is all right.

He rolls over onto his side and stretches his legs. "Go away." He wonders if she heard but knows she must have when, a moment later, the shadowy feet move away from the door. He wants to sleep again, sleep like he has since he got home. When he's awake, he thinks too much and if he's thinking, he remembers.

He doesn't want to remember. He just wants it all to go away.

He wants it to be like it was before. He wants to get his life back.

His sister's voice comes into his head, soft but firm. "Time heals everything. But you have to be patient."

Time. But time is relative and if you keep remembering over and over again, it's like time hasn't gone anywhere. Maybe she's wrong. Maybe there are some things that time can't heal. They're just too big, too incredibly painful.

His eyes are stinging, thick with sleep, but he closes them anyway. He closes them because when he does, time goes back and he's happy again. He's in love and he's being loved and all that's fucked up and wrong with the world hasn't touched him.

~ o ~

The morning dawns bright and beautiful. She loves that her window faces southeast. Even if she can't go out in it, at least she can still enjoy the weather when it's pleasant like this.

She's been up since five and watched the sun rise. The days are getting shorter, but not noticeably so yet. Her heart aches as she thinks about her boy leaving her again. She's proud of him, she is. She just wishes he'd wanted to go to school a little nearer.

She's a creature of habit. She supposes it comes naturally with old age. Her grandmother and mother were the same way when they'd reached her age, or near enough anyway. She's outlived them both now. Her mum died at seventy-three, her nan at seventy. She'll be seventy-nine next month.

"Good innings," her doctor would say.

"Good innings," she mutters to herself. She reaches for one cane and then the other, hooking her elbows in and heaving her short but stocky frame out of her chair. Her boy wants to get her one of those fancy electric chairs that lifts a person up out of them, but she's told him to save his money for school.

"I'll come up with a cure for you, mum. I'll do it." He'd kissed the top of her head and patted the hair down. Silvery hair now, kept short as she can't put it in cornrows like she had when she was young. Her fingers are curled with arthritis, useless for tasks that involve any amount of detail or precision. She knows as well as he does that there's no cure for old-age. Still, he's a good boy to have offered and a good son to trust that she'll still be around when he's a fully-qualified surgeon.

She shuffles over to the kitchen counter, an obstacle-free path for her stiff figure. She likes to line tea bags up on the counter so she doesn't have to work too hard to get them out of the box. Her boy was sweet, having gone through them to separate the pairs.

"You should get PG-Tips, Mum—they're not stuck together like this. They'd be easier for you to pick up, too."

But she likes her Yorkshire builder's tea. PG-Tips is weak. She needs to use twice as many bags to get a cup the way she likes it. She takes her tea strong, a dash of milk and a spoonful of sugar.

The kettle's already full, her mug sitting on the counter where her boy had left it. He really is a good boy. She wishes he knew how proud she is of him, no matter what.

~ o ~

He looks at the back of the estate agent's head as they drive along. She's talking—he can tell that much, even if he can't make out the words. Her head bobbles around and her hands move quite a bit, although they stay close to the steering wheel. He grunts responses. The woman's tiresome and he just wants to be home—his home—but that simply isn't going to happen.

Next to him the care worker smiles, a look of pity on her face. Always pity. He's tired of it. It's like being an infant but with an understanding that everyone thinks you're utterly helpless. At least an infant actually *is* helpless. It's not like he's in diapers.

He's actually quite proud of his health. Until his hearing started to go, and some days it seems just fine, he'd been fit as a fiddle. As it is, that's the only thing that's bothering him and most of the time it doesn't.

The care worker doesn't know. He's careful not to let on. He looks away, smiling and nodding to the front seat.

The estate agent continues talking, not really bothered as to whether or not anyone's listening. He suspects she's Italian. She uses her hands, has that passion not unlike his wife. It's a shame she's an estate agent, then, and not a good wife to a good Italian man. Of course, it isn't like the old days. Women now, they want independence. They want the husband to stay at home with the child — if they want a child at all!

He knows how it is, knows what sort of grief his own daughter has put him through. Is still putting him through. His son, he had been a good boy. Would have been a good man.

The car swings around a roundabout and turns down a side street. The estate agent stops abruptly in front of a block of new build apartments. "Here we are!"

He hears that all right, her face turned, her tone perky. He smiles. The care worker pats his knee. "Right then. Shall we go take a look?"

The flat is tiny. The kitchen and sitting room are one. There's a bathroom and a bedroom and that's it. It's so small, too small. He detests it and that so much of his furniture has been sold off because of it. Besides that, he saw an Asian woman in the flat across leaving with a baby in a pram. "The baby will keep me awake. And I smelled curry."

The care worker gives him a look he's seen often. He doesn't understand why she looks at him like that. As though he is a child who has spoken out of turn. He wonders why all these women have so much power over his life. Strangers, all of them.

The estate agent doesn't seem to notice his protests. "It's really delightful. And it faces southeast so this apartment gets a lot of sun. It will be just like being back in Italy!"

"I hate the sun," he says.

She turns away, saying something else, and once again his ears fail him. He shrugs, turning back to the care worker, but she has wandered into the bedroom.

"It comes with a fridge, washer/dryer, and even a dishwasher which, for this size of apartment, is quite a nice bonus. Especially for someone such as yourself." The estate agent looks at him as she speaks. He nods, accepting he is not going to be listened to any more than he can hear.

~ o ~

She stretches and rolls over, coming quickly to the edge of her single mattress. Reaching out from her warm duvet, she grabs her phone to check the time. It isn't yet nine.

Rolling onto her back, she yawns, stretching her arms up over her head and pushing them against the wall. She points her toes, flexing each ankle. She's actually feeling pretty good.

She pushes the covers down so they bunch around her waist, exposing her bare skin to the cool air of her room. Cool because she left her window cracked open. A chill wind blew in last night, a sign of the changing seasons and the fast approaching school year.

In some ways she's eager to start back. An idle summer with a brief weekend city break to Berlin has left her feeling more listless than ever. She sometimes wonders what, exactly, she's doing here in this larger-than-life city.

The pleasant smell of coffee drifts in under the crack where her door doesn't quite meet the floor. That would be one of the roommates. Hard to tell which one. Either he nagged her into making it or he'd resigned to getting it himself. Either way, she knows that there will be one cup left over once the two of them have theirs. There always is.

It's like their way of thanking her for doing all the cooking. They both have to work, needing the extra cash to pay for expenses student loans don't cover. During the school year they have little time between study and work, and during the summer they fill their days with extra shifts, squirrelling cash away for the leaner school months.

She is grateful to have a reliable income from her parents, monthly deposits into an account and the substantial savings of her college fund that allowed her the opportunity to study abroad. It means she is able to lie in, stay out late, and enjoy the summer without financial worries looming.

She doesn't mind that all the household chores fall to her when the school year begins, the other two too tired to contribute much. She's not lazy. She also fully appreciates how fortunate she is to have so much provided to her. She can see it on the faces of her flatmates, the stress involved in paying your own way, having student loans, and being faced with a very harsh reality of ten to fifteen years debt, if they're lucky.

One, the boy, is studying design. He's quite talented and quite anal. He's neat, organised, and detail orientated. The girl is slovenly, forgetful, and rather lazy about everything outside of her school work. She's studying fine art. Both are at Chelsea.

There's a sudden tap at her door. She pulls the blanket up around her, propping herself up on one elbow. "Come in."

The boy pops his head around the edge of the door, a small smile on his lips. "Morning. Coffee?"

"Yes please!" She sits up further, allowing him to bring the steaming mug to her. He blushes slightly, able to see her bare shoulders. She thinks it's cute. He's a bashful boy, very sweet and thoughtful. He slips out, pulling the door to as he goes.

He's her type, actually, when boys are her interest. But she has no intention of going there as she knows too well the mess that would cause. It was such a mess that had landed her in London. No, she thinks as she sips her coffee, her romantic escapades are over. She's simply not going to allow her heart to be broken ever again and the surest way to do that is to never fall for anyone.

She huddles on the small balcony of the flat, a fag in one hand. Her other hand is wrapped around her waist, holding shut the wool cardigan her mum gave her for Christmas years ago. It's thin and worn now, nearly useless, but she keeps it for sentimental reasons—one of the few happy memories she has of her mum.

The morning is bright and blue but the sun is on the other side of the building and will be until late in the day. They only get sun on the balcony in the summer anyway. By autumn it has dipped too low.

She's hardly slept. Anxiety crept up on her, keeping her awake all night with its grasp on her throat and in her chest. Her boyfriend had fallen asleep in his chair in the sitting room, the flickering light of the television dancing across his pale face.

She'd left him there and gone to their bedroom, leaving the door open in case he woke. He might call her out for shutting it, claim she was being 'difficult'. She'd switched on her small bedside light and pulled out a magazine to flip through. She was grateful when morning birdsong started. She didn't have to pretend at sleeping anymore; the hold of anxiety always eased off with daylight.

She takes a long drag, wincing slightly at the pain in her cheek, letting the smoke warm her from the inside. She knows she should quit. It was throat cancer that had taken her mum, lung her nan. But the smoking helps. It numbs her, makes her forget, at least for a little while, that everything in her life is always wrong. She closes her eyes and replays the morning.

Emerging from the bedroom, she'd found him as she'd left him, only now his head had tilted to the side and he was drooling. She'd switched off the television and wandered into the kitchen to make some tea. The noise of the electric kettle was what had woken him.

She had thought he'd be fine, grateful even, that she was making tea. Usually when he slept through the night, always because he'd drunk too much beer, he was rather dopey and slow come morning. He might be a bit disgruntled but he rarely, if ever, had any actual fight in him.

Not so today. He heaved himself from the chair with a strange grunting roar, turning to face her. She'd just set two mugs on the counter and was dropping a tea bag in each one, her head down, her back to him. She hadn't seen the look on his face as she'd said, "Tea, baby?"

"Fucking cow." He'd stormed over, ripping the plug to the kettle from the wall, pushing her out of the way to do so. She'd been startled. He hadn't hit her and sometimes he was a bit pushy, but for some reason this felt different. It was like a switch had been flicked in her head. She hadn't thought, she'd just reacted. Her foot lashed out, connecting with his leg as she held her hands up in defence.

He'd seemed taken aback at first. It had only been a few seconds, but her heart pounded in anticipation of what would come next. They'd both looked down at his leg and she'd wished she could take it back. "Jesus, Chelle!"

He'd clipped her, a glancing blow to the cheek. Then he'd shaken his head and stomped off into the bedroom. She'd remained still, trembling all over, one hand on the counter, the other held to her stinging face. She'd stood there as he walked out of the bedroom and into the bathroom. She'd stood there while he showered and when he came back out, naked but for a towel. She'd stood there as he emerged from the bedroom, fully clothed and ready for work. He hadn't said anything to her, just grabbed his jacket from the hook by the door and left the flat with a thump and a bang.

~ o ~

There's a moment, as she wakes up, where she thinks she hears a sound. Her ears perk to listen as her sleep-dazed mind struggles to sort out dream from reality. Something woke her, a shout, maybe?

Rolling onto her side, she looks at her child where he lies sleeping next to her on the bed. He's on his back, his arms thrown out to the side, his hands making little fists. His belly rising and falling with little baby panting. His tiny fat lips are slightly parted.

It's now, when he is still and quiet and her mind is soft with sleep, that she feels unquestionable love for him. Her heart is overwhelmed with it, a rushing feeling of intense longing. She reaches out, holding her hand just above his sleeping form, just so she can feel the heat off of him.

He reminds her of his father when he's awake, when she can see the colour of his eyes. It makes her ache to think of it, focusing her mind on the reality of her situation. She can't look at her child, with all his needing and wanting, without resentment. Too often she catches herself fantasising about running away, leaving him lying where he is, to be found when his crying brings someone to knock down the door. Or maybe she could call it in herself, anonymously, when she's far enough away.

When these thoughts come to her she is flooded with such

guilt. This is why she feeds him sugary things and buys him cheap little toys on their rare trips out—as if she could undo the horrible thoughts with bribery.

She'd had trouble getting to sleep, finally managing to drift off a little after two am. She doesn't know what time it is now. Her dreams were fitful and she's disoriented. The image of the young man next door lying on the floor, possibly bloodied or maybe having heart trouble, keeps flashing into her head. It wasn't unheard of. Just a few weeks ago the papers had been full of stories about a young woman, a runner, who'd had a heart attack. She'd been fit and well, nearly thirty, about to run a marathon.

The phone hasn't rung again and she did hear him when he told her to go away, so he must be okay. She wonders why she's worrying so much about a complete stranger.

But then, is he? Really? She's lived in the flat long enough, seen him around. How distant can we be, she wonders, from the people we live right next to?

She wants to know him. She wants to know anyone. She also needs to get a job. Not because she's lonely but because she's running out of money. She hadn't had much to begin with, and lately the bills have been coming more frequently, and the warnings are more threatening.

But what can she do? She doesn't have money for child care. Her family has disowned her and her friends... Well, she's not had any real friends since she was a girl.

She knows she's stuck in a pattern. Every day the same cycle of thoughts go through her head. Everyday she knows what she needs to do but she can't manage to sort out how to do it.

Moving slowly so as not to wake her child, she leans over the edge of the bed and slides out the tea tin she keeps underneath it. The lid pops off with a metallic twang and the baby snuffles, cooing slightly. She tips the contents into her hand and rolls back onto the mattress. Holding the small wad of money up, she undoes the elastic band, as she does every morning. She counts each bill carefully, first one way, front to back, and then the other, back to front. She peels a single twenty from the roll, replaces the elastic, and puts the roll back in the tin.

She wishes he wouldn't fuss so much and says so.

"I'm not fussing, Ma, I'm just trying to make things easier for you while I'm gone."

"I'm just a bit creaky, I'm not an invalid." She smiles, though, adoring that this child of hers is such a considerate man. She knows too well that men have little reason to be considerate — entitled is more often their attitude, no fault of their own, of course.

He was her little miracle, conceived well after she'd given up hoping for a child. "I know, but that's no reason why you shouldn't feel a bit more comfortable." He comes over to where she's sitting, putting an arm around her and kissing the top of her head.

"I'm comfortable enough. You got me those lovely sticks for walking about and I love these." She motions to the reading glasses that hang around her neck. He'd picked up a new, stronger pair for her after she complained about the tiny print in the papers.

"I know." He squats down next to her chair. "I know you won't consider it but I'll ask again, what if you moved to Edinburgh?"

"Oh baby boy." She leans forward. "My life is here. My memories. I'm too old to settle down somewhere new and not so old yet that you should feel like you have to care for me."

He sighs, his dark brown eyes full of worry. But she knows he is relieved as well. He has a life of his own. She doesn't want him to take on the burden of her care to the neglect of his future. "Besides, what would Adam think?"

At the mention of his roommate his eyes flick away and then back. "Oh, he found a new place."

The worry goes from his eyes, replaced with a new expression, one with which she is familiar. It's his reflective look, when he goes inside himself somewhere. It's an expression she knows from his boyhood, when he had a secret he didn't want her to know. The thing is, she always knows. She's his mother. It's her job to know.

She realises this isn't the case with many parents. Years ago other mothers remarked to her that they were baffled by the inner workings of their children. They felt shut out or confused by their actions, unclear as to what their motivation or reasoning was for doing a thing. She'd wondered if her boy was special or if perhaps she was simply better at paying attention. She supposes it helps that she had no ideas about her son. She had one longing for him only: that he be happy.

His brow is furrowed, the crease reminding her of his father, one of the few characteristics he got from him, as he's nearly as dark as her. He stands up and moves to the kitchen, pressing his hands on the counter and sighing deeply.

She is sad for her boy. She wants to ask him about it but she won't. She has never been one to pry unnecessarily, trusting that a person will open up only when they want to and prying is the surest way keep them from feeling ready to do so.

She looks at his back, strong and muscular under his light T-shirt. How much he's changed since he was little, and yet how much he remains the same, too.

The moment, if there really had been a moment, passes. He opens a cupboard, resuming his fussy manoeuvring about the flat. She watches him, memorising him, although also knowing that she couldn't possibly forget anything about him. He is her world and has been from the moment she learned he was growing inside her.

~ o ~

The flat is quiet now that the roommates have left, her off to work, him off to pick up textbooks for the rapidly approaching school year. As they'd gone there had been a traffic jam of people in the hall: an estate agent and some woman with an old man colliding with her roommates. They came out of the flat next door and didn't fit in the hall with two college students and their bikes. The bikes were a bit of a nuisance, sure, but the old man had been totally unreasonable. He'd waved his arms angrily, shouting something about 'thugs'.

It makes her laugh to think of her unassuming flatmates described as thugs. The guy across the hall, maybe, with a neck thicker than his head, but Franklin and Felicity? At least the estate agent had been nice, introducing the new neighbour as 'Mr. Verdi' and explaining that he'd be moving in over the next two days.

She enjoys these rare times when she has the flat entirely to herself. She never fully appreciated space until she left Canada and came to London. As much as she likes her flatmates, it's been an adjustment living in a single ten by twelve foot room and sharing a common living room and kitchen space with two other people. At least she still has her own bathroom, even if it is right next to the front door and not an en suite.

She emerges from it now, wearing just a pair of blue y-front briefs. Walking around in the near-nude when she's alone is liberating—particularly since her flatmates really are so terribly 'English'. She's reading a book about English-ness and finds it immensely helpful. She considers herself a people watcher, someone with a keen interest in the workings of those around her. It's why she chose to study psychology.

She goes to the kitchen to put on the kettle. The thought of her roommates returning, catching her so exposed, makes her laugh. The scandal of it, for them only, of course. For her it would be added to her amusing collection of anecdotes.

Franklin would be embarrassed. He'd flush red, bobbing his head in that way he does and pushing up his terribly hipster glasses, dodging around to his bedroom to escape. Felicity would probably be unfazed but assuredly talk about it with him later in hushed whispers that she could easily overhear through the wall their bedrooms shared.

It's not like she actually wants them to or anything. She just finds the thought amusing. She is, after all, studying the behaviour of people. She finds people so confusing so much of the time, something that frustrates her immensely. Why do people do the things they do, react how they react and treat others so appallingly so frequently? She thinks of home, briefly, and her heart clenches.

~ o ~

"How have you been feeling?" the doctor says to the chart she she's holding. He's tired, annoyed at having been driven around so much that day—collecting the key for the movers, being brought here, knowing he's only got one night left in his home. But that's to be expected, of course. He's always an early riser but his days are usually more leisurely.

"Fine." Doctors should be seen when one is sick. He is not sick therefore he should not be seeing a doctor. The care worker insisted, though, as she seems to do with everything these days.

He doesn't like this woman doctor with her pinched features, lack of makeup, and hair tight up in a bun. She looks too pale, sickly, almost, and too young to be a doctor at all.

"You've had some problems with your cholesterol. Have you adjusted your diet?"

"Pah." He bats a hand, signifying indifference. He's hearty. He's not been to the doctor for any good reason in years. Just 'check ups', as if any good could come from seeing a doctor when you are perfectly healthy. They make things up if you do that too often. They have to look like they know what they're doing, like they're in charge of your health. Especially these days. He's suspicious of the new things he hears about, ailments and diseases that didn't exist when he was young, all packaged up with pills to take. What happened, he wonders, to getting a bit of sea air?

She raises her eyes from the chart, looking at his chin. "Well?"

"Do you have a husband?"

"We're not here to discuss my personal life, Mr. Verdi. I want to run some blood tests on you, check your cholesterol and a few other things. At your age it's so important to make healthy choices."

"What for? At my age I want to enjoy what little life I have left."

"Also, you seem to have a bit of a wax build up. I'll put in a referral for you to see a specialist. You'll have to follow-up on it but it shouldn't take more than a few weeks."

"Weeks! I know how these things go. It takes months, more like, and no one ever tells you why or apologises for it."

It's as if he hasn't spoken. She gives him a tight-lipped smile before stepping out of the room, saying she's going to fetch a nurse. He sighs, looking around himself at the posters he'd already examined during the ten minute wait before being seen.

The door opens again and a young man enters. "Hello, Mr. Verdi, I'm Kwan. I'm just going to do some blood labs today."

He tilts his head to one side and grunts, raising an eyebrow. Oriental nurses and woman doctors—what is the world coming to?

"I'm here to do your blood work," Kwan speaks louder this time, enunciating his words, quite used to the faded hearing of most of the elderly patients he sees.

"Well get on with it," he unbuttons the cuff of his shirt and rolls up the sleeve, resting his arm on the side of the chair.

"Oh, we won't be doing it in here. We just need to go next door." Kwan gestures, turning away as he speaks.

"I don't want to walk all that way!"

"Sorry? It's just next door, sir. Not far. Do you need a mobility device?" This time he speaks to Mr. Verdi directly, not as loudly as before but clear enough.

"Pfft. Special rooms for things. I just don't see why this room isn't good enough." He sets his mouth in a thin line, standing up reluctantly.

"It's just where we keep all the supplies for this, and we have a special table in there for you to rest your arm on." He leads the way next door, speaking as he goes. Mr. Verdi doesn't hear a thing.

~ o ~

The face staring back at him looks dreadful. He's sporting a fine layer of stubble, a rusty yellow-orange against his pale cheeks, which are more pale than normal. His lips are pale, too. Washed out.

He pulls down an eyelid, inspecting his bloodshot, overtired eyes. Rubbing the sleep from the corners, he steps back and looks around the tiny bathroom. He could shower, brush his teeth maybe.

Getting up off the couch hasn't changed anything, though. He simply doesn't see the point in any of these things. He's not sure how to see the point, at the moment, and wonders if this 'moment' is going to pass or not as it feels rather permanent — despite what his sister liked to tell him with her Buddhist mumbo-jumbo.

Work had called again, leaving messages on his mobile and the land-line he never uses. Concern turned to anger to concern and back to anger again. He's probably lost his job.

There's a knock at the door and his heart thumps in response. He steps out of the bathroom, pausing in the doorway momentarily. His head feels as if it's stuffed with cotton wool. His flat looks dreadful but he barely notices as he walks through to the front door.

Opening the door just a crack, he peers out to see a young, pretty face. A woman with smooth, dark-brown skin. He recognises her as his immediate neighbour, her little boy propped on her hip, pulling at her short black hair. She smiles softly.

"Yes?"

"Uh." The smile dissolves, replaced with a confused furrow of the brow. "I just, I..."

"Yes." His tone remains flat. He knows he looks like death warmed over, even through a crack in the door. He wants her to leave so he can continue to mourn, to wallow, to stay cocooned in this pain. He guesses it was she who knocked before, whenever that was — midnight, maybe?

"I wanted to make sure... If there's anything..." She can't seem to finish a sentence. Her little boy turns, points at him, and lets out a little squawk.

"Hi," he says it without thinking. He loves kids. They're easy, fun little creatures. This one is all cheeks with thick, blue-black hair and umber skin, like his mum. His eyes are bright and wide, a startling hazel, reminding Tim of that famous National Geographic photo of an Afghan boy.

"Say 'Hi', Malik." She takes the small boy's hand, waving it for him. The boy looks at his hand rather than at the person he's meant to be waving to.

"Malik? That's a nice name." He smiles and pulls the door open a little more. "I'm Tim."

"Namisha." She keeps her eyes averted.

Tim looks down at his clothes: wrinkled jeans; an old button-up shirt, untucked and dishevelled; and socks with a hole in each so his big toes stick out. He imagines he probably has a bit of a funk to him now, having neglected any kind of personal care or consideration for quite some time. As if to announce this, his stomach lets out a low rumble that turns into a high squeak at the end. Namisha squeezes her lips together, suppressing a giggle. Tim's cheeks flush as he puts a hand to his stomach.

Namisha asks, "Are you hungry? I have some food."

Tim considers turning her down, but knows his own fridge is empty and now, with someone there to witness it, he's aware of the overall fatigue he's experiencing. The thought of heading out anywhere to get food makes him shudder with exhaustion but at the same time, he sees that he can't simply crawl into a hole and disappear. Despite wanting to be dead, he isn't. So he nods. "Yeah, uh, that would be great."

Namisha isn't sure what compelled her to ask Tim if he wanted food, but now here he is, in her flat. Malik is sitting on Tim's lap, as she prepares to heat up the Aloo Gobi she'd made the previous day.

"I'm really sorry if the phone disturbed you—and him." He bounces Malik on his knee. The little boy stares, his mouth slightly open.

"Oh, don't worry. I was awake." She stirs the pot of food on the stove top, having never liked microwaves. She happily sold the one they had after Malik's dad had left.

Glancing surreptitiously at her guest, Namisha wondering if maybe he has cancer or something like that. He looks very ill.

He also has that smell men get, a sort of musky funk. A smell she doesn't miss and regrets to think Malik will one day bear.

"You have a really clean place," he says. His voice is flat, as if he's reading from a script, speaking simply to fill the space. Malik begins wiggling, leaning away, and he sets him down. Her son crawls over to a box full of toys, pulling them out and flinging them on the floor.

"Thank you." Namisha smiles, letting out a little laugh. "Not for long with him around."

"It's really, um, impressive, actually—considering the kid."

"I clean when I'm stressed. It helps me to think," she says. In the pot, the food begins to bubble, the rich aroma filling the air.

"You, uh, you must be stressed a lot," Tim says. "That smells amazing, by the way."

"Hopefully you'll like it. It might be too rich for you." She takes two small bowls down from the cupboard and sets them on the counter. He gives her a small, tight lipped smile.

"I'm sure it will be fine."

He takes the bowl she brings him, breathing in the steam rising from it. Malik comes across the carpet on all fours, pushing a truck with one hand. It connects with her foot, quite sharply, but she refrains from calling out, instead scooping him up and kissing his head. Malik squirms, letting out little grunts by way of demanding to be put down.

"This is really, really good." Her guest looks up from his bowl, a spoonful halfway to his mouth.

She's not sure what to say so she just smiles, but Tim has already looked away. She puts Malik down, collecting her own bowl of food from the counter and sitting on the edge of the sofa, keeping her distance from Tim. She hopes she doesn't come off as wary or unwelcoming, but she's uncertain about him. He's so thin, so pale and unwashed. He looks broken.

She tucks into her own bowl of food, the first thing she's eaten all day and the same things she's been eating for weeks. Potatoes and cauliflower are cheap and last a long time. Sometimes she cooks soup, thinning out leftover curry until the flavours are muted. Something that might have lasted her two or three days could easily last seven with some extra water and a pinch more salt.

Finished, Tim stands up, pushing the bowl away and startling Namisha from her inward reflections. "That was really amazing. Thank you."

"Oh!" She moves to get up, to clear his bowl, her own bowl of food barely touched, but he shakes his head. Motioning for her to sit, he collects his bowl and goes to the sink.

"You don't have to." She tries to cut him off but he sidesteps her smoothly.

"You cooked. And besides, I'm gatecrashing your home." He washes the bowl and spoon, drying them with a towel hanging off the handle of the stove. More than her husband ever did. More than her father ever did, in fact, or any man in her life.

"Thank you," he says, again. For a moment they both stand there in an awkward tableau. Namisha tries to think of something to say but before she can, Tim excuses himself, thanking her again and saying he should go.

The apartment feels even emptier than usual once he's gone. Namisha sits down at the table with her rapidly-cooling bowl of food. Malik pushes another toy car around the floor, making growling noises in his throat. Namisha's thoughts turn to the shrinking roll of money. A stab of guilt fills her chest as she thinks about what her plans for it had been. It's as if Tim's presence in her flat has reminded her of the world moving on, regardless of her participation in it. She squeezes her eyes shut, trying not to cry. Looking down, she sees the mess of toys Malik has spread across the floor. Food forgotten, she begins to collect up them up.

~ o ~

She really hates the way she looks in the Sainsbury's colours. Orange and purple. Or is it maroon? She's never quite sure. Eggplant, maybe. Regardless, she doesn't like the way the top fits — or doesn't fit — and the colours highlight every little spot on her face. She always makes sure she has a solid layer of foundation on for work so she doesn't look like she's about to sit her A-levels.

"All that gunk on your face makes you look tarty, Chelley," her mum would say.

She pulls a face at herself in the mirror, having just finished with her makeup. She's had to get a bit clever around her eye to hide the bruising. It looks alright though. She's good at makeup, understands how to accent her cheekbones, bring out her eye colour. It's better than anything her mum ever wore. Her mum with her hot pink lipstick and blue eye-shadow.

Her mum would have sided with Darren, of course, come up with a reason why her daughter deserved what happened to her. Her mum had always been like that. She'd said she didn't want her daughter 'getting too up herself', to remember her blue collar roots and where they came from. Chelle never saw what the big deal was about coming from Essex, and neither did the rest of the world.

She's on another closing shift. It makes for a long day. She needs to be at her best. She walks into the living room where she's set her bag and a light jacket on the chair Darren had slept in last night. Picking them up, she scans the room, making sure everything is in order. He always drinks more when she works late. Sometimes it means he'll already be asleep when she gets home, the beer having knocked him out cold. Sometimes, though, it means he's riled and ready for a fight.

She doesn't want another fight. She has to keep the peace.

Slipping on her trainers, she grabs her keys from the shelf by the door. She's leaving a bit early so she can walk to work rather than taking the bus, enjoying a fag on the way. Anything to help her calm down and relax.

She's locking her door when someone behind her speaks.

"Hello!"

She jumps, startled, and turns. Normally the neighbours don't really bother with each other beyond tight lipped smiles or an acknowledging nod. She recognises this girl, no more than a teenager, smiling at her. She and two other kids live in the flat at the end of the hall—students, probably.

The girl carries a huge rucksack, swung across one shoulder

and pulled to the side so she can slip her keys inside an open pocket. "Such a glorious day, isn't it?"

"Yes." Chelle always feels awkward when strangers speak to her, she really wishes they wouldn't.

This girl, American or something from her accent, is smiling at her like they chat in the hall every day. She isn't sure what she's meant to do—she just wants to leave, to go to work in peace, but now she's worried the girl will want to walk with her. She considers pretending she's forgotten something in her flat when the girl steps forward, sticking out her hand. "I'm Darcy."

"Michelle." She doesn't really like her full name, has gone as Chelle since she was about twelve, so she's unsure why she just introduced herself like that.

"I've seen you a few times," Darcy says, "but realised I'd never said hello before. Weird, isn't it?"

Chelle nods. She's dying for a fag and just wants to go to work.

The girl walks past her, waving as she goes. "Anyway. See you around."

Chelle hangs back, waiting for Darcy to go through the fire doors before walking slowly in the same direction.

~ o ~

Darcy isn't usually so forward. In fact, she surprised herself by saying hello to Michelle. It was the sort of thing she might have done when she was younger, still living in Canada, but she's learned quickly that the English don't think of speaking to strangers as 'appropriate'. When she'd first moved here, last year, she'd spoken to the woman in apartment 204 a few times— helped her with her shopping, that kind of thing. She's an old lady, really sweet, and seems to be mostly on her own. Her name is Hester, which Darcy finds very fitting.

Everyone else in the block of flats 'kept themselves to themselves', as Franklin would put it, and soon, so did Darcy. Now, beyond a smile or a head bob, her communication with the other people on their floor is limited.

She is eternally grateful for Kate Fox. Reading her book helped her understand and adapt to the 'stiff upper lip.' Not a prudish sense of humour or snobbish tastes, but a general societal belief that you don't bother other people and that actually saying 'hello', offering a handshake, or making a compliment to a stranger is considered bothersome, if not downright rude.

Darcy isn't usually one to conform and she supposes it was an act of rebellion when she decided to introduce herself to Michelle. It's one thing to acknowledged and adhere to the age-old tradition of not speaking on the tube under any circumstances, but something about the way her neighbour stood there, hunched over as she locked the door, compelled Darcy to introduce herself. She saw how Michelle flinched when she'd said hello, as if someone had hit her. From the thickness of the makeup around her eyes, it looked as though someone had. Darcy hopes she might have made the other woman feel a bit safe. Like she was someone Michelle could talk to, if she needed it.

Now, waiting for her bus, standing across the street from the apartment building, she watches Michelle walking up the road. She clutches a bag under her arm, moving her legs swiftly, a trail of smoke winding out behind her from the cigarette she's holding. She has wavy, bleach-blonde hair, just past shoulder length, the roots showing dark against her scalp. Her Sainsbury's uniform is ill-fitting but Darcy assumes no one looks good in them.

As Michelle disappears over the bridge that crosses the tram tracks, Darcy begins piecing together her analysis, a habit she's gotten from her studies. What's Michelle's motivation? What sort of childhood did she have? What habits has she formed which are now holding her back? But most intriguingly, had her boyfriend given her that bruise under her eye?

~ o ~

The setting sun catches the bottom of the clouds, lighting them up bright yellow and pink, the sky a dusty orange. It's an autumnal sunset, a quality of light she only sees this time of year. It's as though the rays of the sun are reflecting the turning colour the leaves will soon be showing. Small pleasures like this—simply having a window from which she can view the Lord's great creation—she counts as blessings.

Jacob has been gone an hour already, but the flat still hums with his presence. Everything is tidy. He's done small, thoughtful things, like leaving an assortment of new magazines around on side tables and next to her bed, taking out the bin and compost, and picking up a fresh loaf of bread from a bakery.

His thoughtfulness reminds her so much of his father and now that he's gone, boarding a train to Edinburgh, she sits with the familiar heartache his absence always causes. It's a thing they don't tell you about when you first become a parent: this permanent ache you will carry when your child is away from you. An ache that does not ease as they grow and become an adult. But of course there's all the joy, too, which they do tell you about but which is ineffable. Knowing she's nearer the end of her life than the beginning, she appreciates all this so much more than she ever did in her youth.

From beneath the low coffee table she slides out, with considerable effort, a plastic bin. From it she removes a large, square scrapbook. It's a clever sort of design, she thinks, where a person can add pages as they go along. When she'd first acquired it, the week Jacob left for medical school in Edinburgh, there had been only ten pages to fill. Since then it has grown steadily, page by page, as memories have come to her or she's found old photos hidden in the pages of books or the bottom of shoes boxes.

Flipping through the pages pasted with photos and scrawled on in her shaky handwriting, she comes to the next blank sheet, where she adds another entry using the fountain pen she keeps clipped to the front page. She puts the date along the bottom of the entry, signing it with just her first initial. The pages are all rather new but look yellowed with age in the autumnal light streaming through the window. She keeps the album carefully packed away in the sealed plastic bin so no further damage will come to newspaper clippings or photographs held within. He's never come across it when he's been visiting. He's respectful; he never goes into anything unless she asks him to.

Despite knowing this, she is also aware that she keeps it there in the hope that he might stumble across it. If he does, then everything will be out in the open. If he knows her secret, if he knows the truth, then maybe he'll feel brave enough to tell her his own secret. If she's learned anything in her life, from her faith, from her experiences, from all her losses, it's that love is nothing to be ashamed of. Jacob is the embodied proof of that.

~ o ~

He's always hated moving. He hates it even more when it's being forced on him — hates how often decisions seem to be made for him these days, as though he is a child and not a grown man.

"The moving company has taken care of everything," his care worker said, as if this makes being forced to leave your family home easier. And they hadn't actually taken care of everything. They'd been rude to him, surly and unhelpful. There had been two of them. One was beefy and bald, his arms peppered with crude tattoos. The other had been sinewy, about six foot, and he moved strangely, twitching as if he were being electrocuted every so often. Mr. Verdi wondered if he was on drugs, suspected they both might have been. The tattooed one must have been in prison for a time. He had the look of a criminal, especially because of the artwork on his arms — not that Mr. Verdi considered it artistic, of course.

He asked them to put the furniture in a certain way and they had just scoffed, ignoring his protestations as they continued unloading their van. They left all the furniture against the wall by the door, blocking the path to the short hallway that leads to the bedroom.

At least they had put the boxes in their appropriate rooms, according to what was written on each in thick, black marker. But still, he now has to empty them. He doesn't understand. If he's such an old man who needs telling where to live, why doesn't he also need help in unpacking?

He shuffles around the furniture — a couch, a large easy chair, two sets of bedside drawers one on top of the other — manoeuvring through the gap to the hallway and down to the master bedroom. *His* bedroom, with an en suite — the only toilet in the tiny flat. This is a feature that displeases him immensely. He's never going to be able to have guests as the idea of anyone walking through his bedroom to go to the toilet assaults his sensibilities.

The bed is set up, more because they'd had to than because he'd asked. It was simply too large to leave with the rest of the furniture. The frame is wooden, a sturdy oak piece with solid headboard and gilded leaf carvings. His wife had chosen it when they were first married, and he hadn't hesitated to buy it for her.

He recalls the first time the frame had been moved, when it had come from the store to their front door. It was their first home, where they would live for some years before the children meant more space was needed. A time when everything had seemed possible and old age and death were so far off as to be unfathomable.

At that time their thoughts had been on starting a family. They'd come to London from Manchester so their children could go to better schools, get stronger educations, and be more involved in 'English life' as his wife said. He'd longed to return to Italy but knew that she was happy here, that she wanted what was best for their as of yet unborn children. The two of them were so young then. So full of life.

He remembers their first night in this bed, those first few months in their new home, their whole lives stretched before them, an unquenchable sense of possibility. The memory is so vivid he can almost forget the time between. He runs his hands over the old mattress, which is not as old as the frame but old enough. It creaks as he sits on the edge of the bed, the springs stiff and cold. Closing his eyes, he takes in a deep breath. For a time he lets himself think only of his wife, as she was then: her dark brown eyes; her full, rose-coloured lips against pale skin; her face framed with bountiful, dark curls; her soft accent, uninfluenced yet by the clipped English accent of the home counties. He recalls their wedding, a small affair for both their Italian and Catholic upbringings. An influence, he supposes, of leaving Italy to go to University in England. Not many of their family could come, of course. That had been a different time, when flying wasn't so easy—although he doesn't consider flying to be any easier now. There's all the waiting involved, the tedium of security and luggage collection, the impossibly uncomfortable seats. And the people. All those people crammed into a tube, coughing and listening to music too loud and putting their seats back into your lap. If he found flying easier he would simply go back to Italy, back to the place he always loved best, the place he wishes, almost every day, that he'd never left.

His wife's eyes come to mind and he remembers how easy it had been to say yes to her. How he'd wanted nothing but her happiness, even if it meant sacrificing his own. He is grateful that no one is there to see as the tears slip down his cheeks.

~ o ~

The club had been a bad idea. Tim isn't sure why he thought it would help, but after Namisha fed him he'd had a sense of momentum he'd not had in days. He'd felt stuck, like the world was continuing on around him and he was frozen in a single moment, but her act of kindness was like an invitation. After eating, he'd returned to his flat, showered, put on something he thought was pretty nice, tidied up the place and then—foolishly, he now knows—decided to 'go out.'

He realises, as he stands there, that the moment he'd wanted to escape hasn't gone anywhere. It's still there, just as raw as it was when it happened, just as pure and sharp. The ache in his chest surprises him. He hadn't realised heartbreak could feel so potent and wonders how anyone can function when they've been left—or, more pointedly, told to leave.

It's almost worse here, with the dance music and bright lights. Pretty boys dancing, couples kissing, partners smiling as they move around under the disco ball and lasers. The thudding bass of the music feels oppressive to him, makes him focus in on his aching heart. And that's just the physical. In his head, the thoughts keeps cycling, like a skipping record.

He slips outside into the cool night air. It hits his skin, waking him up and sharpening his senses. Bringing him more into this moment, instead of the other one. There are too many people out here, too, but at least it's not confined like the club.

It's busy, always busy in Soho on any night of the week. There are the tourists, of course, but there are also the Hen dos and Stags—roaming packs that go out regardless of work the next day, unwilling to skip out on this ritual Tim finds incredibly peculiar. He's always wondered at it. This strange, heterosexual tradition adopted by his own community now. He questions it, questions what it means about the person you're marrying or the relationship you have with them when you need a 'last burst of freedom'.

He closes his eyes to feel the gentle breeze more precisely, as well as to shut out the crowded street with black cabs creeping along and packs of people stumbling off the pavement into the road. He wants to embrace the sensation of it across his cheeks, his closed eyelids, rushing in through his nose.

He can't go back inside but he also doesn't want to go back to the flat. He thinks of work, thinks he should call them. He will call them. First thing in the morning. He knows he's lost that contract. You can't just not show up for several days and expect them to hold your job, even if your heart is shattered and you are numb to anything but the pain. It's not just the grief, of course. There's something else now, ever since he ate. It's a tremor of anger, an underlying frustration at his inability to change things. At not even being given the opportunity to fight, to make things work.

He stumbles up the road, trying to block these thoughts but feeling overwhelmed by their sheer volume. In an attempt to derail them, he thinks again of Namisha and her small act of kindness. For a moment his mind calms as he takes comfort in the memory of eating a bowl of rich, flavourful food and playing with a small child.

The negative thoughts are strong, though, and persistent. Soon he is considering how intolerant she would be if she knew the truth. Would she be so kind if he tells her who he is? Who he loves?

He looks around at all these smiling faces, people laughing and holding hands, stumbling around drunk, and he can't imagine that they have ever felt a pain quite like this. This is the worst of the thoughts because it's this thought that makes him feel numb. It's this thought that lays him out flat for days and he knows it wouldn't take much for him to return to that catatonic state.

He doesn't want to think about it anymore. He just wants to go home—and that's the other problem. The tiny flat had long ceased to be where he lived. It was there as an office space mostly, by the end, somewhere he could work when he was 'working from home' and needed quiet. He misses the place he came to think of as home, a home that had nothing to do with a space and everything to do with the company.

After her fifth closing shift in a row, Chelle wants nothing more than to get home and crawl into bed. She lets her head rest against the bus window, not minding the vibration that will probably leave a goose egg. It had been a particularly long shift but now she has two days off in a row, a mid-week break during which Darren will be at work and she'll have the flat to herself. She's looking forward to relaxing, although she knows there will be some cleaning to do. At least the shopping is done: a collection of bags sit at her feet and on the seat next to her. Staff discounts help.

She rings the bell for the next stop and heaves her dead-tired body from her seat, gathering up the groceries in a susurrus of plastic. She's one of only three passengers and the bus driver, familiar with the night shift, breaks the usual stand-offish code of London by bidding Chelle goodnight from her enclosed box up front. Chelle bobs her head in acknowledgement as she steps off, her hands full of bags.

As she crosses the road to her apartment building, a ginger bloke comes down the pavement on the left. He's wearing a T-shirt and jeans, his hands crammed into his pockets and his shoulders hunched up. He looks cold, although the evening is actually quite pleasant considering the time of year.

Chelle realises he's going to the front door and just as suddenly realises he's the man who lives in apartment two-oh-one, on the same floor as her and Darren. They reach the door at the same time and Chelle gives him a shy smile.

"You're in two-oh-three, aren't you?" he asks, punching his code into the keypad by the door. It buzzes and he pulls it open, gesturing for Chelle to go in first.

"Yes. And Thanks." She steps inside and he follows, standing next to her as she pushes the button for the lift with one knuckle. Her hands are streaked red and white from the weight of the groceries.

"Late shift?"

"Yeah," she says.

"Rough."

The lift doors open and once again he lets her get on first. She casts him another smile, too tired to offer much discussion.

"I was at a club." His voice is flat.

"Oh." She's unsure of what to say, what he might want her to say.

The door to the lift opens and she steps ahead of him, just wanting to be home, but the fire doors are hard for her to manage with her hands full so she has to wait for him to pull them open. She's relieved when he says goodnight and slips into his flat.

Inside her own flat, it's dark except for the glow of the clock on the microwave. The bedroom door is open a crack, the sound

45

of Darren snoring coming from the other side. She gently sets the groceries down on the kitchen floor, too tired to lift them onto the counter. She's slow at putting them away, keeping jars and tins from clunking to as not to wake the ogre. 'Ogre'—she used to call him that lovingly in the beginning.

She'd thought Darren was sweet then, and in some ways, he had been. He had been sweeter than any of the others, definitely nicer than her last boyfriend, although he doesn't look it.

Darren is thick set—broad in the shoulder and chest, muscular but not in a body-building way. He shaves his head, fine, soft-brown stubble growing in, the occasional grey hair showing here and there.

Darren could be gentle, too. He likes to cuddle, to wrap her up in these big bear hugs that make her feel so safe. But at the same time, he's intimidating to other men. She had liked this about him until she realised it was even more intimidating when it was directed towards her.

She gathers up the plastic bags, squishes them into a tight ball and shoves them in the bin. She's frustratingly wide awake. She's usually so tired after a late shift she just crawls into bed and passes out.

She slips into the bathroom, deciding to take a shower. She looks at her face in the mirror. Touches her cheek. The bruise doesn't hurt anymore, although she sees, as she wipes away her makeup, that it's still noticeable. Her mother's voice comes into her head: "If you don't smarten up you'll end up alone."

Chelle wonders what it might be like, just her in a flat on her own, no Darren, no boyfriend at all, not even a roommate. She wonders what's so naff about being alone. If it would really be all that bad.

~ o ~

For several weeks Namisha has been convinced she's being punished. Without doing anything, she committed an unspeakable act, simply for *wanting* to run away. He left before she could, of course, and she saw this as a reckoning for her daring to be so indifferent to her own flesh and blood. She'd accepted the punishment, accepted it as something to be taken on and carried.

This was why she hadn't been about to go get a job, why she was slowly spending the money she had saved, as if using it up would be her penance, restoring some balance.

But now she's broken her isolated vigil. She invited another human being into her prison, offered him food, made conversation. And it's changed things. The flat is no longer a prison, or perhaps not the prison it had been. She can see that she's allowed out.

Malik sleeps and Namisha sits on the edge of the bed. She looks at him and then down at the wad of bills in her hand. She's been sitting like this since the early hours of the morning. Noises in the apartments on either side of hers roused her from an already light sleep. She doesn't mind. She's happy to be rid of fitful dreams, dreams which make her feel more tired than a lack of sleep would.

She's considering her options, realising that she has options. This place as a prison had always been self-imposed, or possibly a creation of the voice of her father, a voice she carries with her despite her best efforts. Despite her resentment. Her entire life she's been told what to do, how to act, how to stand, what to wear, when to speak. She's deferred to others, and when she had a moment of thinking she could make her own choice, it had been snatched away. Or so she'd convinced herself.

As the light of day touched the sky that morning, her nervous energy began to manifest itself as something entirely new. She still has enough money. She knows that. Knows that her plans do not have to be so altered; she simply needs to find the nerve again. It had been there before, she can find it again. She just needs to rethink the entire thing. Instead of leaving him with an incompetent parent, she could leave him with someone who might actually have something to offer, something more than she does.

She thinks of Tim: the way he held her son, played with his toys, spoke to him. He could be perfect. Or he might not, but either way, she trusts that if she leaves a note, slips it under his door along with the key, she will not worry. She wants to believe this more than she's wants to believe anything else, and as this belief takes root, some force begins to push her into action. After so many weeks of just existing, she's letting herself catch up with her movements, her desires, her aching want for things to be different.

There's a pad of paper in a drawer. Namisha pictures it in her mind's eye. She just needs to find it, find a pen, an envelope. Standing up abruptly, she doesn't consider the suddenness of her movement, the way the mattress jiggles. She's single-minded now, the decision made. All her plans have come back, slightly altered, but possible again.

She's in the sitting room, looking through the drawer of a side-table. She's got the pad of paper in hand along with a pen, the money clutched in her other hand, when there's a piercing wail from the bedroom. Namisha swallows hard, her resolve no less firm for all the noise Malik's making. It will be like tearing off a plaster, or perhaps more like breaking a limb and then setting it. Painful at first, but with time it will heal. It will be okay. She will find a way to forgive herself, to carry the guilt, and she'll be free.

Malik's squalling increases in volume. It's mid-morning now, but still, she worries about the neighbours. Such a noise will make her escape impossible. They'll wonder too soon, before she can put distance between herself and this building, this road, this city. The crying undulates, a growing and falling wail of such incomprehensible grief—fear, perhaps, almost as if he knows what she's planning to do.

Some instinct is at play and she drops the pad of paper, the pen, the cash. She walks swiftly into the bedroom, stoops to pick Malik up, holding him to her chest and patting his back in comfort. Almost instantly his crying drops to a whimper. He slips a thumb into his mouth, resting his tear-streaked cheek on her shoulder. His little body shakes with deep, shuddering breaths.

She realises what she'd been about to do and the guilt and shame of it are so overwhelming that, as Malik begins to hiccough, her own body shakes with silent sobs.

~ o ~

Hester decided to go collect the post after her morning tea, but once downstairs the outdoors had simply been too tempting.

She's been on a nice walk, probably more of a walk than Jacob would have liked her to take, but she feels much better for it. She's taken her time and hasn't gone far, knowing she'll never hear the end of it should she take a fall. She doesn't ever think she will, of course, but one must still be careful. The walking sticks help, and for Hester it's been wonderful to be one of the first people out enjoying the day. There are lovely shops around Wimbledon, but the High Street is often too busy, and crowds of people tire her out. Of course, these days she can't manage to get that far—even if she did, she'd not have the energy to make her way back. She loves Wimbledon Common, too, with its broad, rambling pathways and thick, bushy overgrowth, but that's even further than the High Street.

Instead, she's gone around the back of the building and taken the path along the river Wandle. It isn't a proper river, of course, not like the Thames, but it is pleasant with its own charm. Hester appreciates this bit of wilderness passing through her end of Wimbledon.

Hester makes it a few metres up the path before her knees begin to ache. She finds a bench to sit on, where she can rest for the return journey. She sits there for a time in quiet contemplation. After ten minutes or so, she eases herself back onto her feet, pulling her shawl tighter around her shoulders. Letting her walking sticks lead, she heads back to the apartment.

In the lobby, Hester opens her little post box and collects what lies within—a few fliers that will ultimately end up in the recycling bin but always manage to take up residence on her counter for some time—and shuffles towards the lift. When she emerges on the second floor, the young woman from across the hall is standing there, waiting to get on. She's clutching her small boy in her arms and his chubby little face so reminds Hester of Jacob at the same age that she impulsively reaches out to stroke his cheek. His mother doesn't seem to mind. Her eyes are glazed and, for a moment, Hester considers asking where the young woman is before simply saying, "Good morning."

Hester has rarely spoken to her neighbours, despite her wish to have more people to talk to when Jacob isn't around. In the years she's lived here she's seen the apartment occupants change quite a bit, but this young woman, with her little boy, reminds Hester so much of herself that she feels an affinity for her.

The girl nods and then her eyes focus, first on Hester's outstretched hand and then on her other hand, which is holding the fliers and gripping both her sticks at the same time.

"I hear him kicking up a fuss, sometimes. I remember when Jacob was his age. It's hard to believe that they'll grow to be men, but they do. And then you'll miss when he was like this, but you'll never forget it.

"Tell me, what's his name, then?"

"Malik." When the young woman speaks, her voice cracks slightly, as though she's not spoken in some time.

"Malik? That's a wonderful name. He really is a lovely child. Gosh—it makes me wish I had one of my own again. Although I'm far too old now, of course. Still, a grandchild would be nice," Hester says wistfully.

Malik begins to squirm in his mother's arms and Hester realises the lift doors have shut. "Oh, I am sorry. Look at me, wittering away and you're off somewhere important, no doubt!" She looks the two of them up and down, making an assessment. The other woman's eyes look bruised and her jacket is crookedly buttoned.

Hester nods, stepping to the side and pressing the button for the lift. "Anyway, you have a lovely day, dear."

As she walks to her door the ache in her knees is quite sharp. She's going to make herself a cup of tea, put her feet up, and catch up on Holby City. Jacob got her one of those fancy TV gadgets so she can fast forward and rewind her shows, and save things for watching later. Hester's considering if she might have some biscuits, too, as she juggles flyers and walking sticks along with her door key, when she feels a light touch on her shoulder. She's surprised to turn and see the young mother there, Malik still squirming in her arms.

"My name is Namisha," the younger woman says.

"Oh! How foolish! We do that, don't we? Ask names of children and dogs but not the person with them. I'm Hester, love."

"We're not actually... I'm—you weren't keeping us from anything."

"Oh?" Hester's knees ache. She's terribly tired and wants to sit, but she can tell this young woman is just as tired. "How would you like to come in for a cup of tea?"

~ o ~

Gian holds the receiver to his ear, listening to the tinny ringing. It sounds as though it's coming through cotton wool. He switches the phone to his other ear, even though it feels uncomfortable on that side, simply so he can hear a bit better.

"Hello?" A clipped voice answers, cutting the next ring short.

"Ofelia!"

"Oh. Hi."

"How are you, sweetheart?"

"I'm a bit busy right now. Work, y'know?"

Despite his poor hearing, he picks up the clicking of fingers on a keyboard. "Yes, yes, of course. No time to talk to your old papa."

"No, none at all. Are you settled in alright?" Ofelia asks with a sigh, as an afterthought. Gian doesn't understand this reluctance she has in speaking to him. Ofelia used to be such a good girl, calling once a week to talk to him and her mother. Now he can't seem to talk to her unless he calls her himself, and then she rarely picks up.

"Well, I suppose. The movers didn't help very much. They seemed to think an old man can move everything on his own."

"Mmmm." Her tone has changed, the clicking sound increasing.

He presses the phone tighter against his ear. "It's tiny. Too tiny. There's an Asian across the hall. Stinks up the place with curry. And a bunch of kids living next door. Students, likely to party and keep me awake."

"Mmmhmm."

"The doctor says I haven't got long." He throws it out there, testing if it gets a reaction.

"Mmmm. Look, I really do have a lot on at the moment. I'm in the thick of it. I'll call you later, when I'm done work, okay?" She sounds as if she's reading off a script.

"Yeah, yeah," he sighs. This call will never come and later, if he asks Ofelia why she didn't call, she'll deny having ever promised to. She'll say she's been busy. She's always 'being' busy. He wonders what the world is coming to when a daughter is too busy to speak to the person who raised her.

They say their goodbyes, hers perfunctory, his cut off as Ofelia hangs up before he's finished.

He sets the phone down and walks to his big leather chair. The movers had come back the afternoon of the move, claiming that they'd said they would, and put things where he asked them to, mostly.

The room is too small for the furniture he's insisted on keeping, so it's no more manoeuvrable than it was when everything was piled against one wall.

Closing his eyes, he recalls many times when he sat in this very chair, surrounded by his family. His son playing with an aeroplane model on the kitchen table, his daughter studiously working through a text book, and his wife—his stunning, wonderful Bella—bringing him a fresh cup of her best coffee, made just the way he likes it.

~ o ~

Darcy drops her rucksack on the floor in front of the door to her flat. It lands with a thud, the many textbooks inside hitting each other and the ground with considerable emphasis. She's fiddling with it to get out her keys when the flat next door opens and the elderly man who caused such a ruckus a few days before emerges.

"Hey!" She gives him a winning smile and small finger wave with her free hand. The keys jangle cheerfully as she pulls them out and holds them up for him to see. She has a policy to kill people with kindness if she can. This guy, Mr. Verdi was it? Is a grump, but she's going to take the higher ground by being as nice to him as possible.

"Hrm," he grunts, nodding his head and touching the edge of the cap he's wearing.

"You've just moved in, haven't you? I was wondering when they'd finally rent your flat out." Darcy slides her key into the lock and pushed her door open. "Anyway, got stuff to do. I'm sure I'll see you around."

He furrows his brow at her, nods ever so slightly, and then turns, walking down the hall. Darcy rolls her eyes at his retreating figure as she scoops up her bag.

Inside the flat, Franklin is sat on the sofa, a silver laptop balanced on his knees. He looks up as Darcy dumps her bag unceremoniously under the coat rack. "How was your first day?"

She sighs. "About the same as every first day of school ever experienced by every student that ever lived: Chaotic, noisy, and generally pointless."

"Sounds brilliant."

"Totally was," Darcy says, walking over to join him on the couch. "And what are we working on?"

"I got my first brief today. A brief but no client description. We get to decide what the company is and come up with our own pitch."

"Sounds fun—but nothing like real life?" She leans in to see the screen better.

"Not particularly, no." He taps away with a stylus on a tablet balanced on the cushion next to him. Darcy doesn't bother asking if he means it's not particularly fun or not particularly like real life. The screen is filled with a larger-than-life graphic of a shiny, green bean, a small sprout sticking out of the top and the words 'Big Bean' underneath, in a dark grey.

"Looks good. So it's a logo design?"

"Yeah. I'm pretending it's a consultancy. They help companies grow their business."

"A consultancy. Good plan. They'll have more money to spend

on a re-brand." She yawns and stretches, looking towards the kitchen where the dishes have piled up. "When will Felicity be home?"

He shrugs in response, absorbed in the fine details of his logo. Darcy heaves herself up from the too-soft sofa and reluctantly goes to the sink. As it's filling up with soapy water, she pulls out her phone and checks Facebook. She's flipping through her feed when a photo catches her eye. Instantly, her throat feels thick and a shot of adrenaline goes down into her stomach. She swears softly under her breath and Franklin looks up. "You okay?"

"Yeah, yeah." She double taps the button and swipes the window away. Her heart beats heavily in her chest. "I'm fine."

~ o ~

Tim clears the messages from his phone—fewer than he thought there would be. In fact, they had all been from the company he was doing work for, and the tearing off the plaster bit of returning their calls, informing them that he wouldn't be back and that he fully understood he was in breach of contract, had been done.

Despite the fact that he'd not been there long, only a few months, they had wanted him to stay.

"You know, we're willing to discuss this. We pride ourselves in flexibility around personal circumstances," the woman who headed up HR had told him. The very thought of having to explain his absence, his total lack of communication for several days, made him feel sick. He'd apologised again, thanking her for the offer and doing his best to make it sound like he was just too embarrassed to come back.

He never works anywhere for long. One of the things he likes about freelancing is that he isn't anywhere long enough to get stuck in on all the office politics. He doesn't like intense social situations. He thinks of Uni, of the small circle of friends he made there—people he still considers friends despite the way life has scattered them across the globe. They're friends he's not really stayed in touch with, but trusts they would pick up right where they left off.

He considers calling one of them, any of them, or maybe going on Facebook and sending them messages. He's not a huge Facebook user. It's too much like being in school again. He only has an account at the insistence of his sister, and he can't actually remember the last time he logged in. He doubts he'd remember his password.

His throat feels thick, tight, and his eyes are stinging. Despite how heavy he feels, how heavy everything feels, he walks to the couch where he curls up on his side, his arms wrapped around his middle, his phone clutched in his hand. He'd never been comfortable in social situations, never really felt okay talking to people he didn't know, until Jack.

It had been Jack, the way he'd made him feel so safe, the way he would carry a conversation without expecting Tim to say anything, the way he'd listen when Tim did have something to say. Jack, with his winning smile and easy way of chatting with strangers, asking them about themselves, showing such interest. Tim had always felt so proud to be next to him, to be the one he'd chosen.

Tim pulls out his phone, unlocks it, and opens the photos. He taps the album he's been avoiding and the screen fills with thumbnails of a face he doesn't want to believe he'll never kiss again. As he begins to scroll through them, the tears finally come.

S he knocks on the door of 204 and stands back. Malik
is standing on her right, unsteadily, his hand clasped
in hers. He squirms, pulling away and leaning towards
their own flat. The door opens a crack, Hester's smooth, brown
face peering out. Her lips spread in a wide smile of recogni-
tion and she swings the door open. Despite having been inside
Hester's flat just a few days before, Namisha is hesitant to enter.
She doesn't want to impose, even though Hester was the one
who offered to babysit anytime.

"Oh good! I was expecting you, but one can never be too
sure," Hester says, as though she's read Namisha's mind. She
puts her hands on her knees, leaning towards the boy. "Hello,

Malik! We're going to spend some time together today. Just you and me!"

Malik pulls himself into Namisha's legs, grasping at the dark material of the dress trousers she's wearing. She wants to look employable. Hard-working. Serious. She's also dressed in a soft pink blouse and a wool coat, which, despite some pilling on the shoulders, she thinks looks quite classy. Her son peeks one eye out from around the back of her knee, gazing at the elderly woman.

"Come on then, baby boy." Hester extends her arms but Malik merely clings tighter, burying his face in the material.

Namisha is surprised at this. Usually he's friendly with strangers, eager to show them his toys or to wave at them. But then, that's out on their brief shopping trips, when he's in his pram and they are going straight to the Sainsbury's and back. Namisha realises she's never actually left him before, not at all. She's not sure if this thought is comforting or distressing, as she slips her hands under his armpits and lifts him up.

Hester steps back from the door and Namisha carries him inside. She sets him and the bag of toys and nappies she's carrying on a circular carpet next to a coffee table. "I'll only be a few hours. Maybe three at the most. I promise."

Hester shuffles over, standing next to Malik, who is already distracted by several trucks he's pulled from the bag. "You take all the time you need, sweetie. I know what it's like to be a single mum.

"This world hasn't made it any easier since I was young, and Lord knows the government won't help. It takes a village to raise a child, they say. And they're right. It really does. But these days that doesn't seem to be how we operate. Or at least I find that people don't live by it like they used to, despite it not being any less true today than it was years ago. I suppose we forget the truth of these sayings because we say them so much!

"The least I can do is give you a few hours peace. Besides. It will be lovely for me to have some company. With my Jacob gone up North, it does tend to get lonely."

Namisha nods. "Of course. I just don't want this to be a burden to you."

Hester waves a hand dismissively before asking, "So, where are you off to first in your hunt for a job?"

"I have one official interview, but otherwise, I'm going to pop into the Job Centre and see if they can help me with my CV," says Namisha. She steps towards the door, which Hester left open. "I promise I won't be very long."

"Take all the time you need. We'll see you when we see you." Hester settles herself into her easy chair, giving Namisha a little wave. Namisha waves to Malik, who doesn't notice, and steps out into the hall, pulling the door shut behind her.

She will come back, she tells herself.

~ o ~

Tim's flat feels tiny, claustrophobic. Without a job to go to, he has nothing to distract him. There's something about the obligatory tasks of work that provide comfort. He can switch off a lot of his brain, or rather, he can direct it so single-mindedly to the task at hand that anything else is simply forgotten for the time being. His sister says it's mindfulness, which is a buzzword these days. Whatever you call it, though, he misses it. Misses the comfort of being focused on something he's good at, something that might present challenges, but is entirely uncomplicated.

He cycles through his earlier conversation with his last contract, their insistence that they were willing to listen, to hear him out. He wants a job but not one where they have any ideas about him. Something entirely new to lose himself in because while it feels easiest to just curl up and ignore the world than to try to function in it, he's still living, even if it doesn't quite feel like it.

He looks around his apartment for something he can focus his mind on and spies the overflowing bin.

Gathering it up, he marches out of his flat and down the stairs at the opposite end of the hall from the lifts. His footsteps echo in the enclosed, white-painted space as he trots down. He pushes the emergency exit door open and steps into the courtyard where there are larger collection bins for the tenants—a green bin for recycling, a black one for food waste, and a big yellow one for everything else. His neighbour, the woman from the night before, is there, shutting the lid to the green bin. He walks over, casually tossing his own bag into the yellow bin. "Y'alright?"

"Yeah," she says, pushing her hair behind her ear.

"Working again tonight?" he asks.

"No. It's my day off."

"Ah, that's nice." He pushes his hands into his pockets, looking down at his bare arms. "You must think I'm hugely impractical. Always coming outside without a jacket."

She shakes her head, a light flush of pink coming to her cheeks. "Not at all. It's not that cold."

She's what Jack would call a 'chav'—a side of him Tim doesn't like but a memory that stings none-the-less. There is something about her that says she's rough around the edges. He supposes it's the style choices, not just the bleached hair with dark roots showing, but the feathered, slightly-out-of-date cut, the Adidas track bottoms, the oversized button-up shirt that's probably never been ironed. She looks particularly tired, too. Without make-up, he can see the bags under her eyes and noticeable blemishes across her cheeks. Tim feels guilty at these thoughts and supposes this is why he says what he says. "Uh, I'm not, uh working today either. Or at all, actually, at the moment. Would you like to uh, have a cup of tea?"

~ o ~

Hester was delighted when Namisha said she'd consider her offer to babysit. The young woman explained that she was alone and needed to find a job, but couldn't afford child care. Hester had been careful not to ask about the husband—or partner, she didn't know if they'd been married. She'd not seen him in some time. Fathers don't have the same accountability to a child that the mother does, so she isn't surprised. She hadn't asked about Namisha's family either. She didn't want to assume anything, of course, but brown girl, white boy. It didn't take much to guess that Namisha's family probably hadn't approved of the match.

Now that the ten month old is tearing around her apartment, his earlier shyness overcome, Hester remembers how much work a small, energetic child can be. Jacob had been quite studious and calm, a gentle and thoughtful child, but not until around the time he turned five. Before that he'd been the same bundle of energy Malik was proving to be, able to go for much longer than Hester could keep up with. Not that she'd been young when Jacob was a child, but she was considerably younger then than she is now.

"Now then, Malik. What are we going to get up to?" she asks, trying to follow his trajectory. Malik, scooting around the coffee table, suddenly stops, turns, and blows a raspberry at her.

"Would you like a biscuit?"

"Bik-it! Bik-it! Bik-it!" Malik sticks his arms straight up in the air, pumping his hands into little fists and releasing them in star-bursts.

Hester pulls herself to her feet and shuffles to the kitchen counter where she keeps a ceramic jar full of ginger snaps, Garibaldis and digestives. Jacob scolds her about these, saying they have too much sugar and she should be careful. It always makes her smile when he scolds her like that. How the child becomes the parent.

She brings Malik a digestive, giving him half to start with. He's sitting on the floor now, running a truck back and forth on the floor, smacking it into the leg of the coffee table.

Hester settles into her chair again, nibbling on the Garibaldi she grabbed for herself, remembering what it was like to mother a small child, instead of a grown man, as though it were yesterday.

Jacob had been such a surprise to her. At her age she shouldn't have been able to conceive and bear a healthy child, and yet she had. She believed that all children were, in their way, miraculous, but Jacob really was a near impossibility, biologically speaking.

She hands Malik the second half of his biscuit while he's still happily munching what little of the first half made it into his mouth. A collection of crumbs have scattered on the floor where he sits, and his fists are covered in a sticky cookie mash.

"Jacob liked his biscuits as a boy too," she says. Malik looks up at her, a hand to his mouth, his cheeks bulging as he chews.

"Just like his daddy. Just between you and me." Hester leans in, looking to either side so Malik will know she's telling him something in confidence. "His daddy wasn't the man who raised him. Not that his father 'raised' him much. I've never told anyone this, of course. It's between God and me. Although I want Jacob to know, one day."

Malik looks at her, his dark brown eyes wide, his expression earnest, and says, "Bik-it!"

~ o ~

Chelle follows Tim up to his flat, surprising herself by making comfortable small talk. She tells him she has two days off in a row. She's relieved after so many closing shifts, of course. When she goes back she's got some mid-day shifts before another close. Chelle's not sure why she's telling him any of this, but she knows she's not keen on returning to her own empty flat.

After seeing Darren off and having her morning fag and cup of tea, Chelle felt a sort of anxious energy at the prospect of the day stretched before her. The flat was cluttered—cups and empty bottles left on the coffee table and floor, stacks of old maga- zines and free papers from the Underground, plates covered in crumbs, bits of laundry strewn here and there. She'd picked up a stiff sock left next to one of Darren's shoes, made a face. She'd wanted to enjoy the day but the obligation to clear up weighed heavily on her, as well as a deep resentment.

Darren just wants to come home and put his feet up. Darren works so much harder than her. His job is demanding. As if, thought Chelle, as she'd assessed the mess, five eight-hour shifts in a row with one fifteen minute break and a half hour for a meal from 4:30 to 11:00 aren't demanding. On her feet too, because the chairs they give the cashiers hurt her back. She deals with a near constant flood of after-work shoppers for the first half of her shift, then a slow, maddeningly dull drizzle for the second. Never mind spending her shifts with people she dreads turning into. They remind her of how her mother was—missing teeth, thinning hair, stiff dark hairs sprouting from her chin.

When she thinks of it, Chelle feels claustrophobic, as if time is running out on her life amounting to anything of significance.

Like motherhood. Just before her mum died she'd go on about how Chelle needed to pop out a kid soon or it would be too late.

In a fit of frustration at the mess of the flat and her life, Chelle whirled around in a flurry of activity. She loaded the dishwasher, collected up the laundry, stuffed the bin full of trash. She gathered up the recycling to take outside, telling herself she wasn't doing any of it out of obligation. But she knew it was a lie, and that was why, when Tim invited her up to his flat, she was so eager to go—to get out of the stupid pattern she always let herself get stuck in, as if her life was a script she couldn't help but follow.

She doesn't tell Tim any of this, of course. She's happy to talk about her schedule. Chelle fills the silence with insignificant details and facts from her job. She's surprisingly at ease as he unlocks his door, letting her step in first.

"How long have you lived here?" she asks, finally directing the conversation to him.

"Four years? Nearly?" he says.

"Funny we've never really chatted before. Why do you think that is?" She sits in one of the two chairs next to the tiny, round kitchen table and looks around the space. It's an identical layout to her and Darren's flat. There's art on the walls, though, and all the furniture—including a desk with the tallest legs she's ever seen, a sharp-edged sofa and the kitchen table with two chairs—looks like it just came from a showroom. She also notices a lack of television.

"Don't know really." He fills the kettle, sets it on its base and flicks the switch to start the boil. "I guess it's just how things are. Community isn't what it used to be, maybe? That sounds a bit trite, doesn't it?"

"Maybe." She picks at a loose thread on her track bottoms, unsure of what to talk about. "So...uh, what do you do then?"

Tim chews his top lip, hesitating for a fraction of a second before saying, "I'm between jobs at the moment."

"Oh. And when you're not between jobs?"

"Programming, coding."

"Sorry?"

"Software programming, web design, that sort of thing."
He holds up his hands and waggles his fingers, as if he's at a
keyboard.

"Oh!"

They lapse into a silence Chelle finds quite awkward, until the
kettle clicks and he invites her to look at his mug selection. Unlike
the classy decor of the flat, the mugs are cheesy. Tim makes her
laugh as he displays each one like he's presenting prizes on a
game show. She makes her selection, a cream coloured mug with
an illustration of a woman on it that says 'A clean kitchen makes
for a happy mum!'

He chats as he prepares their tea. "So how long have you
worked at Sainsbury's?"

She shrugs. "A few months. I was at Boots before that. Had a
run-in with my manager and had to go. I used to work at a salon
when I was younger but the chemicals bothered me."

"Fair enough." He carries their mugs over to the table, putting
hers in front of her. "And Darren, was it? Your boyfriend? What
does he do?"

"Construction. He's a carpenter."

"That's a good job."

Their banter is relaxed, and the ease Chelle felt earlier returns.
He's kind of posh but not in a way she finds off-putting. In fact,
he's entirely unlike most of the men she's used to. He asks her
more questions, and she's surprised at how easy it is for her to
answer, how okay she is with his enquiries, despite being a virtual
stranger.

~ o ~

"Where are you going?" Felicity asks. She's laid out across the
sofa, her food tipping dangerously close to the edge of the plate
balanced on her thighs. Franklin, sitting next to her in a far more
upright position, leans forward, placing a finger on the edge of
the plate and pushing it up.

"I want to welcome Mr. Verdi," Darcy says. She stands by the
door, a small basket filled with an assortment of things hanging
off of one arm.

"Who?" Franklin asks.

"The new neighbour," Darcy says.

"That guy?" Felicity pulls a face, "Why?"

Darcy shrugs. "Dunno. Just because. Seems like a nice thing to do." She doesn't say it's because she's trying to practice compassion. She knows what Felicity is like. Her response will be flippant, like Darcy is being a flake.

"Is that, like, a Canadian thing then? Taking baskets to the neighbours? Very 'Anne of Green Gables'," Felicity says.

"I think it's a good idea," says Franklin, much to Darcy's surprise. He eyeballs Felicity's plate, which is starting to droop again. "Thanks for cooking dinner, by the way."

Darcy recognises this tactic. Franklin employs it often—he disagrees with Felicity and immediately changes the subject. It doesn't always work, often turning into a snarking session. Darcy smiles and slips out the door before this is likely to happen.

She does wonder about the two of them sometimes. Franklin is such a sweetheart. So put together, gentle, and unbelievably patient. She suspects it's his patience alone that sustains their relationship. Felicity is a mess, emotionally and in the way she fills a space. She's a typical art student, really: disorganised, cluttered, and easily distracted by shiny things.

Darcy taps on the neighbour's door with her free hand. The basket she's carrying was in the communal closet by the front door, some remnant of an Easter long past. It's pink and plastic, cheap looking because it is. She did the best she could to improve it though, arranging a few bags of tea, two clementines, and a small bar of Green & Black's chocolate in some white tissue paper. She came across the basket whilst doing some cleaning around the flat—something she'd been doing to distract herself from going online—and spontaneously came up with the idea of putting something together in it.

The door opens a crack so she can only see a sliver of Mr. Verdi's face, one watery blue eye beneath a scowling brow and stiff set mouth. He grunts in a questioning way.

"Hello sir. We met the other day. I just put together this little basket to welcome you to the building."

He doesn't open the door any wider, eyeing both Darcy and the basket with suspicion. "You're dressed like a boy."

Darcy looks down at her jeans and white button-down shirt, pretty much the only thing she ever wears. Her hair is freshly cut for the start of school—short sides and back with a quiff at the front, reminiscent of a 1940's military cut. She smiles, despite herself, and says, as pleasantly as she can, "I suppose in a way I am, if you believe there's such thing as boy's and girl's clothes these days." She holds out the basket. "For you!"

She's surprised when he opens the door some more, reaching to take it. He looks at the contents and smiles, sort of. The way he has of keeping his lips squeezed together makes it look more of a grimace. Darcy hopes her own smile doesn't convey the sarcastic monologue running through her head.

"So... Welcome to the building then," she says.

He nods once and shuts the door.

"Wow," says Darcy. She goes back to her own flat where Felicity and Franklin are still sat on the couch, although their plates are now washed and in the drying rack next to the sink.

"How did it go?" Franklin asks.

Darcy shrugs. "Felicity was right. That probably wasn't one of my best ideas."

"Told you," Felicity says. "Some people are just ass-holes."

Franklin rolls his eyes towards his girlfriend and casts Darcy an apologetic smile.

~ o ~

"How lovely," the care worker says, spying the basket on the counter. "Where did this come from?"

Gian glances over and mumbles that the neighbour brought it over.

"That's practically unheard of these days. You must have really appreciated the gesture."

He considers the item, one he finds intrusive. He picked through it yesterday, inspecting the contents carefully. His doctor said he couldn't have chocolate anymore—his risk of diabetes was considerably high and he was lucky to have dodged it until now. The teas were horrible herbal things, and besides, he doesn't drink tea. And the oranges? What sort of a man nibbles on fruit to fill his craving?

She dresses funny, that girl. Her hair is too short. He doesn't understand it, allowing women to wear slacks. These days girls seemed to look more like boys and boys more like girls. It's like the seventies again—he sees boys with long hair, down to their shoulders, wearing tight jeans. It all makes Gian very uncomfortable. As far as he's concerned, the 'gesture' was an ill-conceived presentation of things he didn't like nor want.

"Pah. Kids. She was probably, how they say on the TV, 'scoping' my house for things to steal," he says. He wants to show this woman that he is not happy and that his unhappiness is largely her fault for making him move to this terrible place.

She continues to beam, not at him but at the basket and says, "It's nice to know you have such thoughtful neighbours."

He wonders, as he often does these days, why this woman feels the need to speak to him at all as she never includes him in her conversations. Anything he says is glossed over or ignored entirely as she continues on her monologue. He considers this ability to babble on senselessly a flaw in most women. A flaw his wife and own daughter thankfully never possessed.

His wife was always sensible. She didn't speak unless necessary, so her words were always relevant and meaningful. His daughter simply didn't talk to him—out of some odd sullenness he imagined was common in teenage girls. As a small child she'd babble happily about the many exciting things she was learning and discovering, but as she grew older, her chatter ebbed. It eventually dried up so much that the few words she spoke were, like her mother's, out of the barest necessity. 'Yes' or 'No' to a question and 'fine' in response to any enquiry to her mood, school, or feelings on what had been chosen for dinner.

As the care worker carries on he feels a sudden longing for

his two strong but silent women, over this babbling parrot. He is exceedingly grateful when, after a few more minutes of inane verbal assault, she says her goodbyes.

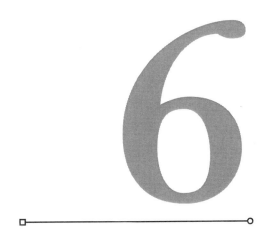

The flat feels different, warmer somehow. Namisha leans against the counter, a cup of tea in her hands, a pot of curry bubbling on the stove. Malik plays in the corner, engrossed in stacking three blocks on each other, climbing a small figure to balance on top, and then knocking the entire structure down by running one of his dump trucks into the base. He repeats this several time, smiling at Namisha after each cycle.

Those few hours of freedom—a brief opportunity to get out and look for a job, have a cup of coffee in a cafe without a squalling baby next to her, to pop into the library on the High Street to take out a book—have rejuvenated her. When she returned to pick Malik up from Hester, she was excited to see him. A sort of relief washed over her at the joy she felt when he crawled over to her, his arms outstretched for a hug. Hester said he'd been a dream, was such a darling, an inquisitive child. An unfamiliar feeling filled her chest, which she only realises now, watching him play, was pride.

Namisha tried offering Hester a ten-pound note for her trouble. The elderly woman waved it away, telling Namisha it wasn't any trouble at all and she actually felt she should be giving Namisha something, as it was so nice to have someone to talk to. She insisted, while Namisha was looking for a new job, that she was more than happy to look after Malik.

"If it's easier on him I can come across to yours. It's not far," Hester said with a wink.

The old woman's kindness was so unexpected Namisha began to cry. Hester took her hand, patting it gently. It wasn't a big cry, more like a small moment of overwhelm, as if Namisha had been numb for weeks and the combination of so many emotions, in such a short period of time, had flipped a switch. When Namisha finished crying Hester pulled a handkerchief from the sleeve of her cardigan and handed it to her.

"Oh, love. It's not right for one person to have all the responsibility of raising a child. I wouldn't have made it through myself if it hadn't been for my best friend coming around to help out sometimes."

Namisha apologised for crying but Hester gently rebuffed her. "It's quite alright to cry. Best not to be apologising for something so natural as having emotions."

Namisha sets her tea down on the counter, checking the bubbling pot of food. Since Malik's birth she's struggled with her inability to warm to him. Everyone says you have this intense emotional connection the moment you hold your baby, but there were so many problems: the difficulty she had with breastfeeding (wasn't it supposed to just happen?), the way she resented him when he kept her awake, the fact that he demanded so much of her. She looks at him again, this whole other person who just doesn't seem to be a person yet.

Malik's picking up the blocks now and dropping them, laughing at how they bounce on the thick carpet. She wonders if perhaps falling in love with your child is as gradual as falling in love with any other person.

~ o ~

Tim wakes late the next morning and for a brief moment he remembers what it feels like to be happy. He'd been dreaming, a dream that felt so real to him it takes a moment for him to even realise he'd been asleep. The sensation, the safe, warm glow in his chest, the lightness in his thoughts, lasts about two minutes or so. Then the thoughts start up, a flood of information to remind him that his partner kicked him out, his future has been ripped away from him and today would have been their third anniversary.

He squeezes his eyes shut, trying to pull back the sensation of being happy, a feeling born yesterday while having tea with Chelle. It had been nice—like he was playing a part, pretending at being normal, stable, whole. Chelle found him funny, laughing at his silly jokes. The sound seemed to chase his grief from the corners.

He hates that this hurts so much. He knows it shouldn't, knows it's not such a big deal—or shouldn't be such a big deal. So many people are dealing with so many worse things, he thinks.

On the night-stand, his phone suddenly begins buzzing. He swipes the screen, not even bothering to look at who it is. "Hello?"

"Oh. My. Gawd. You picked up!"

He winces at the familiar voice of his sister. "Hey, Rachael."

"'Hey, Rachael'? Seriously? That's your answer? Gone practically AWOL and all you can say is 'Hey, Rachael'?"

"I've not been AWOL," he says, rolling onto his stomach and propping himself up on one elbow.

"Seriously? I saw Jack change his relationship status and then you go totally off the radar for like, days, weeks practically. And then suddenly, yesterday, you update LinkedIn. Didn't occur to you to maybe check in and let people know how you are?"

"How do you think I am?" he snaps.

Her voice softens. "Hey. Look, I know it's shitty. I know. But silver linings, right?"

"You are fucking kidding me, right?" He hangs up the phone, dumping it on the mattress.

Jack had been right about her, she was an insensitive slag. Tim had tried, of course, to maintain a relationship with her, but she was just so pushy and opinionated. It was almost a relief when Jack told him he didn't like her. He'd been so upset about it too, had cried, the poor thing. He'd told Tim it was hard because she was his sister and he really wanted to try to like her. "I don't like the way she talks to you, though. She's controlling. Always telling you how you should live your life."

Tim couldn't cut her out entirely—that would have felt wrong—he'd just put in less of an effort to see her, made excuses about having too much work to do, that sort of thing. He was glad of it. If this was what Tim could expect of her now, when his heart felt like a pulpy mess, then good riddance. He didn't need someone like Rachael in his life, someone who was supposedly so 'compassionate'. He had other people he could rely on, people who would understand, who listened and didn't tell so much.

~ o ~

Hester scans her flat, hoping she's not forgotten anything important, and then feels a bit silly. She's only going across the hall. It isn't as though she couldn't come back if she needs something not packed into the carry bag slung over her shoulder. Besides, it's just a few hours, and she imagines Namicha will have anything else she might need. She suspects it's just Jacob rubbing off on her. He was very sceptical last night, during their usual weekly phone call.

"As long as you're taking care of yourself too. I don't want you to tire yourself out," Jacob said with concern.

"Oh darling, I'm a big girl, me. He's a delightful little boy - so much like you were at that age. Not at all mischievous, if a little excitable. He wears himself out. I just watch over him."

"Well, just be careful," he said.

"I will, love. I will. And how is school?" she'd asked, knowing it was best just to change the subject.

Still, Jacob's worry seems to be affecting her and so, before going across the hall, Hester takes a deep breath and thanks God for blessing her with a son who cares so much and for companionship in the form of a small boy. Almost immediately her heart feels open and any tightness she was experiencing slips away.

When Namisha opens her door to Hester, she begins telling the young mother about Jacob's call right away. "The poor dear. He does fret over me. It's very sweet."

"I hope you don't feel obligated?" Namisha asks.

"Oh! No dear, I'm quite happy to help. Please don't fret. Jacob just seems to think I'm practically an invalid. I don't expect him to understand how the company of a small child does so much for my own energy." Hester gives Namisha's arm a reassuring pat.

"Well, thank you. Anyway."

"Oh, don't say any more about it. Now, you must have things to do. I don't want to keep you."

Once alone Hester turns to Malik, who is sitting on a blanket on the floor, a bottle of juice clamped between his lips. He sucks it ferociously, watching Hester with his hazel eyes.

"Where did I leave off yesterday?" Hester comes over, sitting down on the sofa. "I was telling you about when I met Jacob's daddy, wasn't I?"

Malik continues to suck his bottle, his eyes focused on Hester.

She's always wondered at how people fail to see the human being in children. They seem to think babies are all the same and personality doesn't come into it until they reach a certain age, but Hester knows better. She can tell that Malik is clever, inquisitive, and not in just the way toddlers are as they learn. He watches her in a way that shows he's trying to figure her out, find out who Hester is. She doesn't believe he'll remember anything she's telling him, which is what makes it so easy to talk to him, but she's careful anyway. You never know what someone's first memory will be.

"I want to be perfectly clear," Hester says. "I believe in the sanctimony of marriage, and I think the world is full of too much divorce. If people knew themselves better perhaps there wouldn't be quite so much of it. I did love my husband for a good long time, even after I found out he didn't love me — that's what a person does if they've gotten married for the right reasons — but I'm not saying what I did was any better than what he did. But always know, the heart is a mysterious thing and love, when it's found, is not something trivial to be cast aside."

Malik pops the bottle from his mouth. "Bik-it?"

"Yes, that sounds like a good idea. We should have some biscuits while we chat, shouldn't we?"

"Bik-it!" Malik laughs, a high chortle bubbling up from his tummy. Hester pulls the jar of biscuits from her bag, continuing to talk to Malik all the while. "So yes. I was a wronged woman, but it didn't make my own wrong any better."

Malik raises a hand, taking the digestive offered to him. He holds Hester's gaze once more as he crams the cookie into his mouth.

~ o ~

Chelle arranges the biscuits on the plate in a neat circle. She wishes she could bake, but she knows an attempt to do so would result in something which would not come across as a gift so much as a punishment. She doesn't want to put Tim off — she's thrilled that he texted her and so glad they had exchanged numbers before she left the day before. She's happy to spend more time with him. It gave such a lift to her day, so much so that it seemed to have rubbed off on Darren. When he got home she already had dinner ready and he was really sweet about that, wrapping her up in one of his bear hugs and kissing the top of her head.

"I really love you, y'know that?"

"I do," she told him, setting the plates of oven fries and baked chicken on the table.

Darren took her by the shoulders, looked into her eyes, and like a shame-faced little boy, apologised. He said he was so afraid she was too good for him, deserved better than him and what he could give her. She apologised too, finding it easy, knowing her own temper was just as volatile. But then he'd said something she hadn't expected. "I drink too much. I know that."

"Sorry?"

"I drink too much and it's not right. Not for you, not for me either, but especially not for you. I…" He looked down, letting his hands drop from her shoulders and hang by his sides. "I'm going to get help for it."

Chelle hadn't really known what to say. She knew so many words were a great effort for Darren. She was worried that if she opened her mouth, she'd start crying, and he wouldn't understand why. So she just leaned in and kissed his cheek, telling him they should eat. They made love that night, in a way they hadn't for a long time, and for a moment, before falling asleep, she wondered if she did want a baby with this man.

That morning he'd been a bit more his gruff self, but Darren was often grumpy when he first got up. Chelle was in a good mood, though, as she saw him off. She had her morning fag and a cup of tea out on the balcony and then came back inside to find Tim's text.

As she carries the plate to the door, she feels a little thrill run down her spine. Perhaps she can't talk to Darren about a baby just yet, but she thinks she could tell Tim. There's something about him, his open boyish face, the way he asks her questions.

Chelle slips on her shoes and steps into the hall, deciding that she mustn't let it bother her. She's just going over to see the neighbour, just going to have a chat — no agenda involved.

~ o ~

"What about rain on your wedding day?" Felicity asks.

"If you were a meteorologist, then it would be ironic," Darcy says without hesitation.

Felicity nods. "Okay, right."

"See, it's not difficult to make the song make sense — like, for irony to actually play a part in everything. It's just, as it is, nothing in it is ironic."

"You could argue that makes the song itself ironic," Felicity says with a tilt of her head.

"You could, but I still don't think that's what Alanis was going for."

The two of them sit on the sofa, facing each other, their backs against the arms and their legs a tangled mess in the middle. Darcy knows she's procrastinating, as so many students are wont to do, but she just can't bring herself to go over yet another highlighted passage in her textbook. This is not a habit she usually indulges in but with Franklin working there's no buffer between her and Felicity, who seems to have a contagious sort of laziness. The two of them are taking turns tapping into the Bluetooth speaker with their MP3 players, sharing and discussing the music on their playlists.

"So what about ten thousand spoons when you really need a knife? That must be ironic on some level," Felicity asks.

Darcy shakes her head. "Nope. Pain in the ass, but not ironic. Ironic if you were in a knife factory, maybe?" She leans her head back on the arm of the sofa, staring at the ceiling, struggling to think of an ironic twist to that particular musical line.

"See! Not so easy. Not everything can be changed." Felicity crosses her arms.

"Well, maybe she'd just have to rewrite that bit ent..." Darcy stops mid-sentence, lifting her head and looking towards the wall. "Did you hear that?"

"Hear what?" Felicity asks, inspecting her fingernails.

"There was a thumping."

"You just don't want to admit that you can't make that bit ironic."

This irritates Darcy, but before she can say anything, the thumping comes again, more noticeable this time. Darcy untangles her legs from Felicity's, getting up to investigate. As she puts her ear to the wall, the thumping comes again, a shuddering bang that makes her jump back.

"What is it?" Felicity asks.

Darcy turns to Felicity, pointing at the speaker, which she now realises is quite loud. "Turn that down."

As the volume decreases, there comes a steady plea, like a mantra, from next door. "Quiet! Quiet! Quiet!"

"Sorry, sir!" She cups a hand around her mouth.

Felicity rolls her eyes. "Grumpy old bugger. It was better when no one lived next door. We weren't playing it that loud. He's just complaining for the sake of it. Like a hobby. I bet he can't even hear it."

The thumping stops, and Darcy returns to her spot on the couch. "Whatever. It won't kill us to be nice to the guy."

"The guy is a dick," Felicity says.

Darcy chooses not to respond. Felicity's self-righteousness really gets to her at times. The way she claims anything to do with being polite or acknowledging other people's opinions is 'oppressive' to her creativity makes Darcy want to smack her. She hates how people see her generation as irresponsible or entitled. Being labelled a 'Millennial' bothers Darcy, and people like Felicity just seem to re-enforce the pervasive belief that their generation is so 'plugged in' they've become indifferent. Immediately after thinking this, Darcy is overwhelmed with guilt. She's trying to be nicer to everyone, but she can't seem to stop thinking so negatively about her own roommate, and despite her best effort, the guy next door is getting on her nerves.

~ o ~

Gian snorts, satisfied he's won, as the tinny sound of the music next door stops. He'll remember to tell that case worker about this when she comes around again. He said this sort of thing would happen. He wonders if they are smoking dope and, if so, how he can prove it. If he has to stay in this place at least he can find a way to get rid of the less agreeable neighbours.

A new family is living in his home now. He knows this because the case worker told him. She seemed to think he would be happy—happy that a home he bought for his wife, where his children grew up, where he'd intended to die for Christ's sake, belongs to someone else now. He doesn't see why the value of a house should be directly related to how much space you take up in it. It wasn't too big for him, not that anyone bothered asking. It was the youth in this country. Everyone who made decisions for him was younger than him and seemed to think they knew better somehow.

It's just like when he was made to retire. He worked his way up at the London Brick Company, was comfortable as a manager and happy to stay in the position. Gian stands by the kitchen window that overlooks the courtyard, reflecting on the day they told him his time was up. There was a letter on his desk declaring their appreciation for his years of service but, according to company policy, he had reached the age of retirement, and wasn't it great that he'd now get to spend more time with his family?

It was as though they'd forgotten what had happened to his family—or perhaps they hadn't. Maybe they remembered all too well. He knew his performance had suffered. He'd not been making his targets, but he hadn't missed a single day, outside of the one he'd taken for the funeral. He supposed they thought it would be better for him to be home with his wife and daughter, to be the glue of the family and spend time with them. Everyone always seems to know what is best for other people, but no one can sort out their own messes.

He'd been given six months to train a replacement—but Gian knew it was because they needed that long to prove he wasn't fit for work anymore, so it could all be done legally. He'd seen them talking to Human Resources, seen the Senior Managers—in title only as they were no more than forty—meeting to discuss what was to be done with Gian Verdi.

He sets his jaw, pushing down against the lump in his throat, leaning heavily on the counter. He looks out the window but doesn't see the courtyard, or the sky, or the little patch of green. Instead he sees his own home, his garden, and he longs for Bella. He longs for her strong arms and kind face. He wishes she were here with him, and that they were in their little brick Victorian terrace home.

D arcy knows she should be back at the flat working on her assignment or, at the very least studying, but she just can't concentrate. It's too easy to go online and get lost in the black hole of social media—not to mention risky. She figured that the best thing for it was to get away from her computer, take a walk, to really think about the essay she has to write.

They're studying Ronald Fairbairn's object relations theory, or 'splitting'. Their assignment is meant to help them explore how the dichotomy of black and white thinking develops according to experience. Darcy has long been fascinated with how strongly held religious beliefs affect the way people approach the world and thought this was a great perspective to use in exploring the subject of splitting. But now she wonders if perhaps she's bitten off more than she can chew. Darcy's got the basic gist of the approach she will take from one sentence she wrote in her notes: What does it mean to hate the sin but love the sinner?

She understands the problematic issue of not being able to see both negative and positive qualities existing together in a single person. It's why she's been trying so hard with Mr. Verdi. Unlike Felicity's assessment, he can't simply be an asshole. There must be more to him, as there is to anyone. But she feels like she's been told her whole life that people are either good or bad, so what does that say about her own mind? This is the thing about studying psychology, of course, the thing people warn you about. You start diagnosing yourself left, right and centre. As you learn all these new theories and studies, you can't help but find ways they apply to your own behaviour and patterns of thought. Just this week Darcy has diagnosed herself with narcissism and borderline personality disorder. She just can't seem to shake the mental hypochondria of being a psychology student — so she considers this walk to have therapeutic qualities, as well as contributing to the formulation of ideas.

She can't help thinking, two years into her degree, that an awful lot of psychological studies seem, ironically, to employ splitting. Someone does a study that says 'This is the definitive reason why people behave this way' and then a bunch of other people set out to prove or disprove that study and attack each other over whose results are 'right'. Darcy thinks anyone with half a brain should be able to see that any pattern of human behaviour has multiple contributing factors.

But then, as she finds a bench to sit on, Darcy wonders about her motivation to leave Canada, to run away and avoid. Darcy supposes she's grown up a lot since then, but she can't really know. Has she just compartmentalised it all, as if her life in Canada could be neatly placed in a box and ignored? As if whatever contributed to everything there hasn't just followed her here? Does she really believe she's put it behind her? If she has, then why doesn't she visit home? Why doesn't she give into her parent's regular requests to see her, their offers of a flight back to Calgary?

Darcy sighs and looks up at the sky, trying to remember more of her notes, to focus her mind on the task soon to be at hand. She wishes the neurotic thoughts away, smirking at her personal irony.

~ o ~

"Look, I'm really sorry but, it's just, I didn't mean to give you the wrong impression," Tim says.

Chelle rests her head in her hands, her cheeks flushing red. They are sitting at the table in Tim's flat, the plate of cookies between them. Tim leans forward, resting a hand on her knee. "Come on. Don't feel bad. It's not the end of the world."

He'd let her in, smiling and friendly, beaming to see the plate of cookies. "I'm really glad you could come over. I wasn't sure if you had plans."

He made tea, just like the day before. Everything fit, everything felt like it made perfect sense. Chelle thought she loved Darren but then, maybe all that love, all the lightness of the night before was something different about *her*. So when Tim leant over to grab a biscuit she misread it. It was impulsive. She caught his shirt with her hand, bringing her lips awkwardly to the corner of his mouth. And then he pulled back and told her.

Of course he's gay. It was so obvious, Chelle thinks, that he shouldn't have had to say. She's an idiot for not picking up on it. She can't help the tears from spilling over, hot and angry, at Tim for not being what she thought, at herself for misjudging the whole situation, and at Darren for being so difficult to love sometimes.

"Look, Chelle. Don't cry. It's okay. Just..." Tim scoots his chair around so he can put an arm over her shoulder. She hears herself babbling through tears, a flood of words with no real thread. They've built up inside her, and it's like they have to come out now. Chelle's not listening to what she's saying—it's just a stream of all the things she's been worried about for so long—when Tim pulls away and says. "Wait? He hits you?"

She shakes her head, trying to remember exactly what she just said. "It was an accident."

Tim's eyebrows shoot up. Chelle knows what he's thinking and wishes she could take her words back, stop sounding like she's talking from some script out of Corrie Street. "No, I'm serious, it was. I kicked him. He just lashed out. I was being a real cow."

"But he did hit you?"

"Yes but it's the only time he's done it. He's actually, he's...kind in his way. My old boyfriend. He...he did hit me." She wants Tim to understand, to see that this is different, that she knows what it's like to be someone's punching bag, and this is not it. "That's actually how Darren and I met, when my ex hit me. Darren saw him do it. We were at a pub. Darren took him outside, he shoved him against a wall, told him to leave me alone. He was so nice to me. He, he checked on me, found out if I had anywhere to go. I didn't so, I went home with him."

"And you stayed with him?" Tim asks.

"He didn't expect to sleep with me. He made his couch up and everything. He was really sweet." Chelle hates how she must sound, as if she's trying to explain it away, trying to make it alright.

"So when did that change?"

"I don't know. He helped me move out, back in with my mum. But my mum..." Chelle isn't sure how to explain the special sort of Hell living with her mother had been. "It wasn't great, y'know? And he was so sweet. So nice. I let him take me on a date, and it wasn't long, maybe a month? Two? Then he asked me to move in with him. It was just...easy."

"A relationship of convenience," says Tim.

"Sorry?"

"You meet someone, and they seem nice enough, so you go along with it, and then suddenly you've been with them for a year or more because it was easy."

She thinks about this. Is it easy, being with Darren? Sometimes. But it's the easiness she wants. It's what happened last night that she wants all the time.

"And now he's hit you too," Tim says.

"I told you, it was just once and I hit him first," Chelle is quick to point out.

"Fine. Neither of you should be hitting each other, but it still doesn't sound healthy."

"I don't know. I've never thought about it," she lies.

"Regardless. The question now is, what are you going to do?"

~ o ~

Tim walks Chelle back to her flat, feeling a bit silly about it, but not wanting their parting to be awkward. They'd talked for a bit longer, after he'd calmed her down.

"I have been hard on him. I could just, back off a little. We both start the fights, me maybe even more than him."

He wonders now, as she unlocks her flat, how people can be so deluded.

"Are you sure you'll be alright?" he asks.

She smiles. "Yes, it's fine. I just need some time to think. Thank you, though. Really. For not being funny."

"It's fine. No big deal." He shoves his hands into his pockets. "If you need to talk just, ping me a text. I'm happy to listen. Anytime." He hopes he can keep this promise.

Back in his own flat, Tim is right back where he was before Chelle came over. He searches for his phone as a source of distraction, thinking to check his email, see if any of the places he applied to for jobs have come back to him.

There is the usual spattering of spam that makes it through the filter—semi-branded calls to action from banks Tim doesn't hold accounts with. There are a few auto-responses to job applications, thanking him and informing him, due to the overwhelming number of applicants, they will not be in touch if his skills don't meet their needs. He taps on the tab for personal emails and his heart catches in his throat as he sees an email from his sister with the subject: **Please do not delete.**

Hovering a finger over the trash can icon in the corner, he considers deleting it without even opening it. He wishes Jack were here, so he could talk to him, ask him what to do. But then, if Jack were here then the conversation with Rachael that morning wouldn't have happened. Suddenly the phone blips, a text message notification popping up onto the screen. It's Rachael, asking him to please check his email. He turns the screen off, dropping the phone onto the table.

They'd been so close, he and Rachael, closer as they got older, despite the four years age difference. For a long time he'd considered her one of his best friends and had felt lucky for it. He saw how most of his friends were with their siblings. They fought over petty things, were competitive, judgemental. If they spent time together it was out of obligation, not because they actually liked one another.

She'd been his greatest ally when he was coming out. She held his hand when he told their parents. He was eighteen at the time, had just finished his A-Levels and was moving out soon. They'd discussed it at length and agreed, if he moved out before coming out, he could easily just leave it forever. He might hide it from them for the rest of their lives because he was like that. Rachael told him she would be there with him, would stand up for him and make it abundantly clear that they needed to own whatever hang-ups they might have. He remembers how proud he was of her, how grown up she was for someone who was only fourteen at the time.

She'd been there for him through his early relationships. The relationships that didn't last more than a few months. Rachael always knew exactly why and would talk it out with Tim — how one guy was all about sex and his unwillingness to remain monogamous showed a distinct lack of respect, or how another was too self-involved and Tim deserved someone who thought about what he wanted. She never attacked them. Rachael would point out how their insecurities were theirs, their actions made sense from what they knew, but it was better for everyone when the relationships ended. He'd always admired that about her, how she didn't say any of the guys Tim dated in the past were bad, but just a bad fit.

Tim had been so excited to introduce her to Jack. Here was this amazing, mature, attractive, worldly guy — someone who respected Tim, was encouraging and appreciative. And Rachael *did* seem to like him, at first.

Sitting down, looking at his silent phone, Tim tries to think of when he noticed friction between Rachael and Jack. A single moment doesn't come to mind, but rather, a gradual accumulation of personal slights and aggravations.

Tim remembers how he went from being a thread between them to some sort of barrier—a constant peace keeper when he was in the company of both of them. He started to feel anxious about Rachael coming over, or going out with the two of them. They seemed to set each other off and in the aftermath, Tim would have to justify and explain away his sister. It became too much after a while, just too hard, but he wonders if maybe he just hadn't tried hard enough. He wanted them to understand how important they both were, how much he wanted both of them in his life.

Now, of course, he's got neither. Jack is never again going to walk through the door. They will never again share a bed or a meal or go on a fantastic holiday somewhere new.

Grabbing his phone, he swipes the screen and codes in his password. His inbox is still open, Rachael's email at the top. Grief grips him again, as he thinks of how much he's lost. An entire life with someone, a life Tim wanted that Jack didn't. Tim feels the heaviness coming back, a dark weight on his heart and head that makes him want to crawl into bed and never move.

~ o ~

Namisha wearily pushes open the door of her flat. The air is fragrant with spicy cinnamon notes and a hint of vanilla. It's cosy and inviting.

"Oh! Hello dear!" Hester, who had been seated in a chair she pulled over by the stove, gets to her feet. "Did you have a good day?"

"Yes." Namisha sets down her bag and takes off her coat, scanning the flat for Malik.

"He's in your room having a lie-down. Poor thing tuckered himself out. I'm just making some biscuits. I thought he might like some fresh ones instead of my dusty old collection."

Namisha gazes at this woman, who she could easily call her saviour. "Thank you."

"For what dear?"

"I have a job. I got a job, and I wouldn't have been able to if you'd not been here to look after him. I—," Namisha grasps for the right words to express the gratitude she feels and comes up blank. "Just, thank you, so much."

"A job! How exciting! And where will you be working then, love?"

"I'll be doing PA work three days a week for a charity CEO. Just part-time but it's something."

"Oh bless! I was praying for you, dear. I really was. Smart, lovely thing like you. I knew you'd find something."

Namisha sits at the table and looks around the flat, finding it odd to see it so tidy while knowing she isn't the cause of the tidiness. "So, he was good for you?"

"Oh very! We chat, we do. I tell him stories. He only interrupts to ask for biscuits. I hope if I keep telling him my stories he'll start saying something new, but he's still young yet. One shouldn't rush these things. You've never met a grown adult who could only manage one word!"

"Wait, something new?" Namisha asks.

"Yes, something besides 'biscuit' dear. What a first word. Jacob's first word was 'no'—which you might think was a bad sign but really -"

"He talks?" Namisha looks towards the bedroom.

"Well, not so much talking as parroting. That's what they're like at this age. Sponges, soaking up new sounds and popping out anything that sticks. Keeping in mind how important it is not to say the wrong sort of words around them, of course."

"When he speaks...He...What does he say?"

"Just biscuit, dear. Have you not heard him?" Hester pauses her flow of words.

Namisha, tears in her eyes, shakes her head. As the tears began to spill out, Hester comes over to her, putting an arm around her shuddering shoulders. "Oh, darling! Oh dear! What's all this then?"

Namisha stares at the kitchen floor. "I didn't realise. I've never... He doesn't..."

"Darling, there will be more words, so many more words. The first one doesn't matter so much unless you decide it does," Hester says.

"It's not that."

"No? Then what is it? Do you want to tell me?"

Namisha didn't realise until that moment how very much she did want to tell someone. Tell them about every little thing piled up in her head: every fear, every minute of anxiety, every doubt and moment of hesitation. She's not sure anyone has ever asked her, in her entire life, to tell them anything that might imply she wasn't entirely capable and content. She thinks of her ex, her parents, her siblings, even her friends, and can think of no occasion when such a generous offer was given. And she's amazed, as the words spill so easily from her mouth, that she doesn't hesitate to be completely honest.

~ o ~

Hester is crossing the hall to her flat, having just said goodbye to Namisha, when the door of 206 opens. One of the two girls who lives there steps out, smiles at Hester and says hello.

"Hello dear." Hester likes the three students down the hall. This one, Canadian, she's pretty sure—Americans always sound louder to her—helps her with her shopping sometimes. Hester can't remember the girl's name and feels bad about this. She always tries to remember everyone's name, because it's polite and because it helps her combat Jacob's worries about her mental facilities.

"How are you today?" the girl asks. She's had her hair cut again. She always seems to be doing something different with it. Hester admires the tenacity of youth.

"I'm very well dear. How are you?"

"I'm great, thank you."

"I have to apologise, dear, but I've forgotten your name. I know you've told me before. I always think it's rude when people forget someone's name but I think it's silly to pretend you haven't."

"Oh! It's Darcy."

"Oh yes! Like Jane Austen."

"Exactly like that, actually. My parents are English professors."

"Well, there you go then! A simple way for me to remember," Hester says. "Sorry I can't stand about and chat, my old knees aren't up to it these days."

Darcy nods, telling Hester she has to be on her way as well.

As soon as Hester is back in her own home, she puts on the kettle. She always thinks better with a cup of tea in hand.

Namisha's crying had been so neat, so restrained, like an actress in an old black and white film. The tears rolling down her cheeks like perfect jewels, her face soft and open. So much confusion, so much worry and fear held on for so long. It was a wonder the young woman had managed up until then. Hester admires her stoicism in the face of such uncertainty. She also curses the world for speaking in absolutes, frightening the life out of anyone who doesn't fit them.

"It's all different, love, for everyone. There's no telling exactly what motherhood will be like, and there certainly isn't one way to feel like a mother. How it feels to you is how it feels, darling." Reflecting on it, Hester hopes her words aren't mere platitudes. She would hate to be dismissive, she just wants Namisha to know it's okay, it was always okay.

Namisha protested, insisting she really truly was a bad mother. Hester had just laughed. "If you want to see yourself as a bad mother, you're allowed to, but you have a healthy baby boy sleeping in there. He's bright and inquisitive.

"You've gotten him this far and you're doing the best you can, which is quite a lot better than what many people could probably manage in a similar situation. Not to make presumptions, of course, of other people and what they might be doing or not.

Regardless, honey, that little boy is just fine, and so are you."

Hester, lost in thought, ignores the now whistling kettle. She takes a mug down from the cupboard, dropping a bag of Yorkshire tea into it. As she switches off the element, and the whistle dies down, Hester becomes aware of a regular thumping. She has to go into the bedroom to hear it clearly. Hester leans near the wall, holding her breath. The thudding comes again and a small shout, "Quiet!"

She stands up straight, pushing back her shoulders and pursing her lips. With great enthusiasm, she pounds right back. "Lighten up, you old grump!"

~ o ~

Gian is surprised at the old coloured woman's strength. Her pounding is shockingly loud for someone who, for all outward appearances, is so frail. He's seen her with her sticks, walking towards the river or going across the hall to that Asian girl's flat.

He doesn't understand why she can't be more courteous. He'd just lain down for a nap when that infernal kettle started whistling. It was always whistling! That woman must drink buckets of tea, he thinks. He wishes she'd get an electric kettle. It's enough to make him want his hearing to go entirely. It's been oddly better today, to no great benefit. Those kids next door and their infernal music, the old woman with her kettle.

Gian decides to go for a walk to get away from it all. He puts on his hat and coat and steps into the hall, which smells faintly of fags. Sniffing, Gian grumbles about the stink, along with the noise.

Outside he walks along the pavement towards the high street. There's a cafe there, Italian run, where they make a decent cup of coffee. When he gets there he orders in Italian from the man behind the counter. It's not like one of Bella's, of course, but the waitresses are kind, and they do things properly. Their eyes flash brightly, their bodies lithe and young in black v-neck t-shirts and black skirts. He wonders, as he takes a seat by the window, if Ofelia would be more like these girls if she'd grown up in Italy as he and Bella had. How different life would be.

He knows why they didn't go back, of course. There were no

jobs, no opportunities and Bella, bless her, wanted so much for their future, for their children's future. She said Britain had more to offer. They could be both Italian and English here, but if they went back to Italy, they'd just be Italian and not see more of the world, not see other cultures. She liked to say you could go to the whole world, or you could live in London, where the whole world comes to live. She was such an idealist, his Bella. Always saying how important it was not to get stuck on tradition or the 'old ways'.

He doesn't see what's so bad about the way things used to be. Despite the fateful year of his birth—in the very same month Hitler invaded Poland—the political turmoil his parents lived through, the work they did to be able to send him to school in Britain, Gian longs for tradition and the days of past.

The automation of check-out lanes baffles him. He misses the friendliness of shopping at locally owned shops, the camaraderie that comes of being a patron, and also a friend, of the green grocer, the butcher, the baker. Sometimes, for short moments, when he's in this cafe, it's like he's back in a time when there was an agreed upon structure to society, when things were far less sped up.

The waitress brings Gian his coffee, and a slice of panforte, which he knows comes ready-made but he pretends is made by hand. He thanks her in Italian, telling her she's very beautiful. He asks if she has a boyfriend.

She smiles, confusion in her eyes, as she tells him her Italian isn't great. She really hardly understands it.

"Oh! I am very sorry. I thought because of the owner—" Gian waves a hand towards the counter.

"Yeah, *he* does." She speaks with a broad Northern accent, a surprise to Gian. "What did you say? It sounded pretty."

"Nothing," he says. She smiles at him before she ducks away to collect the next order from the counter. Gian looks around himself at the other patrons. A woman with a loud barking laugh sits in the corner, talking to a man wearing those strange trousers with the low crotch. Gian thinks they look like something you'd put on an infant to accommodate a diaper. There are also two girls with incredibly short hair, like that girl next door. And a group of Asians in the corner, talking loudly in a language he doesn't know. Gian sighs, sipping his coffee, and looks out the window at the passing crowds of people.

"**A**lright?" asks Janice. Chelle smiles at her co-worker, who has just arrived at the register opposite. Janice is late and notoriously chatty. If a person isn't careful, they can get a warning because of Janice. Chelle can't afford to lose this job so she keeps quiet. Besides, she's busy thinking.

Darren was in a foul mood again yesterday. She isn't sure if not having a beer after work doesn't make him worse. He's so touchy lately, so hot and cold. As she lay in bed next to him, her mind was a bundle of thoughts and nerves.

"Tsk. Would you look at that," Janice says.

Chelle's eyes betray her by flicking up, ever so briefly.

"A hole!" Janice is holding her own Sainsbury's top out at the belly, pointing to something Chelle can hardly see from where she's sitting. "I'm going to guess that's from my washer. It's a piece of junk, I keep saying. I had a tinker with it, trying to get it fixed. Nothing doing. I need a new one but of course, it's not as if I've got that kind of change lying around."

"Mmmm." Chelle wishes Janice would just get on with setting up her till.

"A shame. A real shame."

Chelle reaches for one of the magazines on display in front of the conveyor belt. She knows from experience Janice is less likely to chat if she thinks you're reading. She flips it open, glancing at the celebrity gossip she used to enjoy as a teenager. It's a magazine her mum bought religiously, and Chelle can't help noticing that it always has the same sorts of stories, just with different names and faces.

She's still uncomfortable about last week when she made such an ass of herself at Tim's. He was sweet enough, about the kissing thing, but mentioning the fight with Darren is what she really regrets. Tim took it all wrong, making a much bigger deal of it than it was. She loves Darren, really, or at least she's pretty sure she does. It's just, she's not so young anymore, as her mum would say. Not so very young and not getting any younger. She wonders if she and Darren should get married. If they were married it might be different.

But then she thinks again about what Tim said, the way he looked at her. His eyes had it written all over them — he was judging her, thought her stupid for staying with a man who would lay a finger on her, even just once, even accidentally. She wishes she'd explained better, had managed to tell him how happy she'd felt for the first year, at least. In fact, it really is only in the last few months that things have been hard. She is a real cow sometimes. She just can't help it, is all. She'll be tired, or they'll both be tired, and one thing leads to another and then it's snipe, snipe, snipe.

"Did you see who's getting divorced just a month after their big, white wedding?" Janice's sharp voice cuts through Chelle's thoughts. She looks at the magazine in her hands, to the article the page is open to, the article which Janice is referring to. Chelle flips it shut, placing it back on the rack.

"They have no shame, really. Too much money, not enough sense."

"Do you have to talk so much?" Chelle asks.

"Excuse me?"

Chelle swivels her chair around to face her till as their manager's voice comes on over the loudspeaker, announcing that the store is open.

~ o ~

"Thank you so much for coming in. We have a few more candidates today, but we'll be in touch on Monday to let you know."

Tim stands, pressing down his suit jacket with one hand and offering the other to the woman who just interviewed him. He thanks her for the opportunity, following the script he's followed all week. It sounds stunted, overly formal and probably pretty forced, but it's the best Tim can manage right now. He is acting, playing the part of a healthy, normal, well-adjusted person. He's trying not to think about how Jack bought him this jacket, this tie, the shoes he's wearing.

The sun is bright today, although the air carries a chill and there's a strong wind caused by the tunnel effect of the buildings surrounding him. The Square Mile is it's own universe within the busy streets of London. It moves to a different rhythm, which Tim has always thought he could feel when he steps into it. A cafe just a road away, nearer to Saint Paul's, would be open on a weekend, whilst cafés in Bank kept office hours. People formed orderly queues and moved with purpose. There is no time for them to mill about looking at the historical buildings they work in. Tourists are pests, only to be tolerated and even then, with a thinly veiled tolerance only adopted around the more historical sights, like the Monument.

It's not Tim's world, although it's one he's spent a fair share of time in. He'd considered not taking this interview when he saw the address, knew how close he'd have to go to where Jack works. But he also agreed to meet up with Rachael today, in London Bridge. The proximity is all very convenient, despite the underlying mix of hope and fear at the possibility of seeing a familiar face. He's amazed at how he has come to hate hope. Without hope, he's certain the pain would abate.

He crosses the road from Gracechurch to King William street and heads for London Bridge. The sun has brought out throngs of tourists, although there is a noticeable chill in the air. It's difficult for Tim to navigate through the clumps of people stopping to take pictures of Tower Bridge and the HMS Belfast. There's a queue forming by a man selling roasted chestnuts from a cart. Tim dodges them all and heads along the riverfront, towards Hays Galleria, where Rachael is waiting for him.

As soon as he steps into the cafe he spots her. She's changed very little since the last time they met up, just over six months ago. Her hair is long, the same orangey red as his, pulled into a ponytail. She's wearing an oversized check shirt and black tights, a pair of classic black doc martens on her feet. She wears very similar glasses to Tim, and his own youthful looks mean they often get asked if they are twins.

Her freckled cheeks beam as she spots him and leaps up from her chair. They hug in greeting, Tim stiff and awkward, Rachael's a fierce squeeze.

"It's so, so, *so* good to see you," she says into his ear.

"You too," he says.

"Liar."

They sit down and for a moment Tim wishes he'd not agreed to come, that he could just walk out and not have to explain or live with the consequences. She puts up a hand, palm facing him and, as if she's read his mind, says, "Look. I don't want to scare you off. I'm going to do my damnedest not to sound like an asshole and I really, *really* do want to know what's up with you and how I can help.

"I love you. That's why I'm here. That's the most important thing for you to know. Or, the most important thing for me to tell you. You don't have to believe it but, I'm saying it."

It does help. They talk for a little bit about his job interview, casually, comfortably. The familiarity of being with someone who has known him his entire life, who knows him in a way no one else could, relaxes him. She's so genuine — always has been — and Tim wonders again at how things got so sour between them.

"So - I heard what happened — or rather, I saw him change your relationship status," Rachael says.

Tim's not sure he can talk about this, or even wants to. Tears prick his eyes as he looks around the crowded space. There are too many people here. It's like the club all over again. He suddenly feels so damn raw, and he can't believe no one can see it.

"We don't have to talk about it. We really don't. I know it will all take time, and I don't want this to come out wrong — although it probably will — but," Rachael takes a deep breath, "I'm hoping that I can finally get my brother back."

Tim shakes his head at her. "Don't. Please don't."

"Honey-bunch, I know, I know you loved him…"

"I love him. I still do. It doesn't stop just because…"

For a moment they both look down at the table, unable to make eye contact, to go further. Tim wonders why he agreed to come, what he thought would happen. "I don't get why you still have to dislike him so much. He's not even around anymore, and you still want to make some…point."

"I didn't dislike him. I disliked the way he treated you."

"He treated me just fine! He took me on amazing holidays, he bought me this outfit, Rachael."

"Spending money on someone isn't the same as loving them."

He gets up, meeting her eye. "Don't call me again. Don't email me. Don't text. Just…leave it."

~ o ~

The girl training Namisha is called Polly. She's Scottish and speaks so rapidly Namisha finds her difficult to understand. She's just finished explaining something about a spreadsheet and her words have disintegrated into a jumble in Namisha's head. Namisha smiles in what she hopes is an encouraging way, nodding confidently for show.

"Well, I'll be just right here." Polly motions to her own desk, across from Namisha's. Namisha is grateful that she can make that much out.

She knows the work will be simple, possibly even tedious at times, but it pays well for being only three days a week.

Hester assures her that she doesn't mind looking after Malik whilst Namisha's working, and now that Namisha can get out more regularly she's finding that she misses her little boy. She always thought absence making the heart grow fonder only applied in romantic relationships, and yet here she is, sitting at her new job and wishing he were there too.

She looks at the task list before her, something to put structure to chaos, to organise and fix. Hester told her about the serenity prayer—about accepting what you can't change, changing what you can and knowing how to tell the difference. She's given up on hearing Malik talk when she's around, resolving that her love cannot be conditional, as her own father's had proven to be.

Hester's kindness these past weeks continues to surprise her. Not that the woman is kind, but that her capacity seems unlimited. She cares so much for Malik, greeting him with unabashed joy. She had Namisha show her how to take pictures and make recordings with her phone so she could capture moments to share with her.

"Jacob showed me a bit when he first gave it to me, but I had no reason to use all the bits and bobs it comes with. I've quite forgotten how to make them work, but if you teach me, then I can catch him in the act. I know it's not the same, but at least you'll know it's not the imaginings of some batty old lady."

She didn't mind, she told Hester, if she couldn't film it. But Hester insisted, and when Namisha came home yesterday, there he was on camera, pumping his little hand open and closed as he asked for a biscuit. Namisha surprised herself by crying, not because she was upset but at the joy of it, of his little baby voice making a sound that was unmistakeably a word. Hester took

Namisha's free hand and gave it a squeeze. Namisha was overcome with a longing to go to Malik, who was napping at the time, to hold him close to her and smell his lovely sleepy scent.

As Namisha wakes up her computer and opens her email she thinks how amazing it is, the way life can change so incredibly much in just a very short time.

~ o ~

Gian replaces the phone on its receiver. The chord is so curled in on itself that he has to tug it free every time he uses it, which isn't often. He accepts that Ofelia doesn't wish to speak to him. She didn't even pick up today.

He is so often restless these days. In their home there was always something to keep him busy—a floor board to secure, a drip to sort out, paint to touch up. The age of it, an early Victorian build, called for regular maintenance, and as a result, Gian had a multitude of distractions to while away the hours of his otherwise empty days.

He so enjoyed working with his hands, the way each little task made the home feel more and more like something he had built himself. It was comforting to look at the carpet running up the stairs, knowing he had installed it, or the working fireplace he had spent an entire weekend clearing out, or a replacement piece of glass in a window pane.

In this tiny, modern flat there's nothing to do besides watching TV, an activity he despises. It's all full of violence, sex, terrible language—and these shows move too quickly. He doesn't know how people don't get dizzy watching them. The scenes cut to new settings and different characters before you have time to understand what's going on.

Sometimes he finds old shows, like The Good Life, a favourite of Bella and Ofelia. Bella sometimes said it would be good for them to move to the country, to get a smallholding like in the show. The fresh air for the children, growing their own vegetables, all that space.

It never happened, of course. London had better schools, better transportation, and he had his job. So instead Bella and

Ofelia would joke together about how they could get a goat for in the garden.

"It would keep the grass short, daddy," Ofelia would say, her eyes flashing with mischief. They threatened chickens too, although Gian thought that would actually be quite nice. A few chickens down at the end of the garden, where their smell wouldn't travel into the house. They could have had fresh eggs every day. It would probably have been good for the children — taught Antonio and Ofelia how to care for animals, where their food came from, a little about responsibility.

He looks out the window at the small courtyard meant for tenants to share. This is what things have turned into these days. Small patches of green space surrounded by buildings to house all the people and all their cars. It's a chilly overcast day, so no one is down there just now. The cloud cover is low, solid and white, but glaring. He tries not to think about his old home, where a new family has probably painted over the colours Bella chose for the sitting room, presumably torn up the carpet runner from the stairs, are maybe keeping chickens down at the end of the garden. He desperately wants to believe that they have left it untouched, but he knows this is foolish. He could go there to find out. It's a way to travel, of course. He'll have to take the District or Circle line into the city, catch the Northern all the way up, but he could go.

Donning his tweed cap, wool coat and old, cracked brogues, he leaves the flat. He doesn't know that he'll even get as far as the train, even, but ruminating in this tiny space lacking any character can't be good for him.

~ o ~

Hester pushes Malik's stroller, enjoying how it works as a support in place of her sticks, and actually makes it easier for her to walk longer and further. They've been to the High Street. Hester picked up some groceries as well as a few books from a charity shop, two for Malik and three for herself. She's feeling a strong sense of accomplishment. Malik seems to be enjoying himself as well. He kicks his legs out so they go stiff and straight underneath the blanket wrapped around them, and then curls them back in, squealing delightedly as he does so. He's bundled up in a little wool coat and hat, a matching set Hester bought for him earlier that week. She supposes this was what being a grandmother must be like and wonders if such a thing is a possibility for her—not that her love for Malik is any less than it would be for her own grandchild.

As they turn the corner she spots the shuffling figure of her neighbour, the old man who moved in a few weeks ago, coming out of their building. She's not seen him since their wall banging match, although she has heard him, or rather heard his television set, booming loudly through the wall. Apparently, her kettle is unacceptable whilst his television is allowed to be turned up enough that it sounds like it's in Hester's flat, not his.

Almost immediately she berates herself for having such unchristian thoughts, but she's grateful none-the-less when he turns heading away from them. She leans forward and talks to Malik, telling him the importance of practising kindness. "Especially with those we find it most difficult to be kind towards. We can't think of it as kindness if we only feel it for people we like. Remember, a stranger is just a friend we haven't met yet."

Malik continues to kick his little legs and squeal, pointing enthusiastically at a flock of starlings overhead.

Once inside Hester puts away the groceries and settles Malik down with one of the books she bought him. He's very solemn when he has a book, she's found. She likes watching how serious his face goes. This, like so many things about Malik, reminds her of Jacob as a baby. It's also one of the things that calm him down, gets him to sit still so she has time to catch her breath. Hester sits and stretches out her legs, pulling up her skirt so she can rub her aching knees. "Shall I tell you more about Jacob, then, little poppet?"

Malik looks up at her from his book, his rosebud lips slightly parted.

"I can't remember how far we got last time. I could probably tell this better if I had my album but that's next door, and I just don't think I can manage going over there just right now, so we'll have to see how well I go without."

Malik claps his hands against the book in his lap and giggles.

Sitting on the District line, heading home, Darcy has the sudden feeling that she's being watched. Glancing up from the book she's reading she catches the eye of a man in a suit, standing near the door. The train is crowded, but she's certain, as he looks away, that he was the one staring at her. He seems familiar to her with his thick-framed glasses, pale skin and carroty hair. When the train pulls into Wimbledon station Darcy follows him up and out and to the same bus stop. She stands next to him, noting that he's considerably taller than her.

"We're neighbours, aren't we?"

He turns, his cheeks flushing pink. "Yes, I believe we are."

"I'm Darcy." She offers him her hand, which he shakes, a bemused sort of smile on his lips. "Isn't it weird to live in such close proximity with someone that you can recognise them on the train, but have no clue what their name is?"

He laughs, although it's not particularly light-hearted. More of a forced bark. "I'm Tim," he says, not bothering to answer her question.

Their bus pulls up and Darcy steps on first, scanning her Oyster card and making her way up the stairs to the top deck. She's pleased to see that Tim follows her, but when she takes the seat at the very front, he goes right to the back. Darcy's disappointed. She wanted to talk with Tim, to find out about him.

When the bus gets to their stop, there are several people between them and he dashes across the street to the apartment complex.

In her own flat Darcy can see, from his shoes and jacket, Franklin is already home, but he's in his room, music on and the door closed. He does this when he needs uninterrupted design time so Darcy goes to her own room and flops on the bed. The universe continues to conspire against her, forcing her to work on this essay when all she wants is a human conversation.

Darcy pulls out her laptop and flips the screen up, where she's left the essay open on the desktop. Scanning what she's written, she wonders why she chose psychology, of all things. Sure, people are interesting, but she could have done an easy subject like Felicity and Franklin are doing.

To hate the sin and not the sinner is to understand that what we equate to 'sin' is merely a state of mind or action, not an inherent quality of the person. We are all laden with 'sin'—more accurately negative qualities—in equal measure, but due to splitting 'sin' becomes a solid concept and mutually exclusive with the 'sinner', thereby creating the categorization of 'good' versus 'bad' people.

The problem with what she's written is that it's too damn philosophical. Not enough psychology, Darcy's professors tell her.

With a sigh, she flips her computer shut. She'll finish it over the weekend. Right now she needs a snack. Besides, it's due Tuesday. She has way too much time to work on it. When it's down to the wire she trusts it will practically write itself.

9

Tim shuts his eyes, trying to block out a flood of memories. He doesn't want to think about that last day in the house, the uncomfortable moment of realisation. He's replayed it so many times in his head he wonders how it's not worn out. Reliving that particular memory is like re-watching the moment in a film when a character makes the wrong decision. Every time you watch it, you know what will happen, but you can't help hoping that maybe, this time, just perhaps, it will be different. Either way, he's tired. Tired of thinking, tired of trying to be okay, tired of not being okay.

He takes off his jacket and tie, undoing the top buttons of the shirt. He remembers picking the jacket out—the way Jack smiled when Tim slipped it on, turned, showed it off. Tim misses that smile. He misses Jack's big white teeth, the slight gap between the front two, the deep lines on either side of his mouth, the sharp edges of his cheeks and the small lines that gathered by his eyes. He misses the way Jack would look at him like he was the most attractive man he'd ever seen.

Rachael has no idea, never had any idea. That was the problem, Tim thinks. She didn't see the little ways Jack was so sweet to him. In fact, they weren't even little things, so much of the time. Jack took Tim out for extravagant dinners, on amazing holidays to beautiful places. He bought him perfectly fitting clothes. When they moved in together, Jack encouraged Tim to keep the flat, use it as his office, and even contributed to part of the rent when he could. He was always supportive of Tim's work, wanted him to do well, to have his own funds.

Tim slumps on the couch, covering his face with his hands. He wishes things were different, that Jack had said something sooner, that they could have worked things out. Tim had wanted to get married, he thought they'd both wanted it. He wanted to build their lives together, adventure together, grow old together.

Grabbing his phone Tim scrolls through his contacts, checking names to find anyone he might call. His contacts are all people he's lost touch with over the last few years. There's no one he's really close with. In fact, he knows it's fruitless. He's always been so introverted. It's hard for him to make that sort of friend, it takes a lot of time. He thinks of the only two people he could genuinely talk to, the only two he has truly ever loved, and begins to cry.

~ o ~

"I thought you might like some, as I suddenly seem to have a lot of them." Namisha holds out the small container of biscuits she put together for Tim to have.

Hester is on a roll with the baking, doing it while Malik naps. The flat always smells deliciously of sugar, butter and flour when Namisha gets home. But they've been piling up, much too quickly for the three of them to eat them all. She was wondering what to do with them when she thought of her neighbour. It had been several weeks, three or four, she thought, since she'd knocked on Tim's door and invited him over. A pang of guilt motivated her to take him some of the surplus biscuits, but now she feels even more guilty. His eyes are puffy, his nose red. He sniffles, his cheeks flushed pink with embarrassment. She doesn't want to pry, wouldn't really know what to say, and besides, Malik is alone in the flat taking his nap.

She says goodbye, telling him he can return the container any time. Back in her flat, she puts on the kettle for a cup of tea, knowing she has some time before Malik will begin to stir.

Her neighbour seems like a lost puppy. She tries not to think too much about what might be happening with him, knowing it's not really any of her business, but she can't help the urge she feels to mother him. The irony of this is not lost on her. She wishes she could be like Hester and just know exactly the right thing to say. She's so wonderful, Hester, the way she speaks about anything that Namisha might be fretting over.

"Everyone seems to think being a parent is instinctual, but I don't believe that at all. It's just not what I've seen. Some people are better parents when their children are adults, dear. I don't suppose I'm one of those—I'm sure Jacob finds me insufferable—but that's just the way it goes. There's not a formula for being a good parent. I suppose the lucky ones of us get one of each, a parent good with little children, and a parent good with adult children."

Her own family fits this. Her father always adored small children. She remembers him taking her to the mosque when she was a little girl, helping her choose a dress and holding her hand proudly. She always felt special next to him.

Children of neighbours, her brother's children, even children of strangers, managed to capture and hold his attention. And then there was his ability to indulge small children in the most tedious or hideous things—re-reading a book for the twentieth time, watching the incessantly loud weekend programming for children, putting up with vomit, poo and poorly aimed urine—something she marvelled at as a teenager. She noticed it in contrast to the way he started to ignore her as she got older, about the time her mum began to listen to her more. But of course her mum also believed in traditional ideas, so it didn't really matter if she could see Namisha's side of things, she still deferred to her husband. It hadn't gone over well when her mum shared with him that their teenage daughter was dating a white boy, even if her mother hadn't thought it was anything to be worried about.

Namisha doesn't hold any anger towards him for it, or at least she doesn't think she does. She pours water into her mug, searching for what it is she does feel. It's tender, small and soft right in her belly, like a little ball of sadness. She thinks that perhaps Tim has his own little ball of sadness and wonders if he's ever noticed it before, if that might help him. Then she thinks this is quite silly. And then she stops thinking, as Malik suddenly begins to wail.

~ o ~

"Fucking kid. He should shut his trap." Darren speaks through a mouthful of food.

Chelle rolls her eyes, not in the mood. He reminds her of that bloke from Master chef, the one who lost all the weight, as he shovels heaping spoonfuls of the ready-made cottage pie she brought home from work into his mouth. He breathes heavily through his nose and washes down mouthfuls with long swigs of beer. He's had three since getting in from work. So much for drinking less, thinks Chelle.

"Maybe you should ease up on the beer."

He glares at her, wiping his mouth with the back of his hand, and takes another drink.

"You're going to get pissed."

"So what if I do?"

Chelle crosses her arms defiantly. She wishes she had the nerve tell him she's stopped taking the pill — throw it back at him as proof that she's got more power than he thinks. She knows she won't though. Going off of it for a day, which is all it's been right now, means nothing. And Chelle knows there's no saying how long it might take for anything to happen anyway. She's been on the pill since she was eighteen. She could always get right back on it, and he'd never know a thing. Besides, it's not as if birth control is 100%. That's what they always said when she was still in school, and something she knows from experience. "I don't want to have this conversation right now."

"Then why did you start it?" he snaps.

She rolls her eyes. "It takes two."

She's not sure why she's provoking him. She didn't picture things going like this. Her plan was to have dinner ready, to treat him really sweet so the night could lead where she wanted it to. If they have a fight now, they're not going to have sex, that's for sure. She knows they'll be lucky to even end up in the bed together. If the fight is bad enough, he'll just go out to a pub somewhere, returning late to sleep on the couch.

He glares at her, and she decides to switch tactics. "We've both had a long day."

He snorts. "What, sitting on your fat ass at a till makes for a long day?"

And just like that, she wonders why she even bothers. "Watching you shovel food into your gob makes for a long day."

She's not going to give him the chance to go any further with this. She moves towards the door, to grab her coat so she can leave. She hears the scraping of a chair behind her but she's committed, she's getting out, going anywhere else but here.

~ o ~

It takes Gian exactly forty-three minutes to do what he now considers his 'daily walk'. He wakes early, around five am, and makes himself a cup of coffee. He drinks it while standing in front of the window, in his pyjamas, looking out at the courtyard. Most of the trees have lost their leaves now, their dark branches like cracks against the sky.

Once he's finished his coffee, he tends to the orchid he bought the week previous. It sits on the kitchen counter, where it can get enough light. It's a small consolation to the garden he used to have, but at least it's something.

Afterwards, he dresses, carefully selecting a button up shirt and corduroy trousers, not that his wardrobe consists of any other options. He takes comfort in the methodical click of the hangers as he sorts through to select what he will be 'just right'.

Once dressed he pulls on his coat, a dark grey one with hound-stooth patterning, and puts a tweed cap on his head. By this time it will be nearer to seven, maybe quarter to or so, and the rest of the apartment building's occupants begin to stir.

The route he takes goes up towards the High Street. He collects a paper from the newsstand next to the station entrance before going to the Italian-owned cafe, where he orders an espresso and a roll to go from the man behind the counter, avoiding interacting with the waitresses. He crosses the road and comes back down on the pavement opposite, sipping his drink and eating the freshly baked, still warm roll, the paper tucked under his arm. He has always finished both the espresso and the roll by the time he returns to his flat, around half eight.

Occasionally he might glimpse another tenant, but he keeps his head down, knowing that if they do say something to him, he won't really be able to hear it. His hearing has gotten so bad on the right side now that he no longer hears even the piercing sound of the neighbour's kettle.

Back in his flat, he sits down in his large easy chair, putting up his feet and opening the paper.

The phone rings, startling him slightly, as he turned it up as loud as it will go in case it rings when he's in the bedroom. Flipping the paper shut he gets to his feet, grumbling about unnecessary interruptions.

"What do you think you're doing?" Ofelia's voice is clipped, tense, as he answers the phone.

"Ofelia! My love. How are you? What a pleasant surprise."

"Oh, my gawd, dad. No. Don't even try to pretend."

"Pretend what?"

"The Ferguson's rang. You can't do stuff like that, dad. It's trespassing, and no one is going to care that you're an old man, it's illegal. You could get charged."

"Who?" He presses the receiver into his ear. The left side is a bit better, but he's only getting half of what she's saying. "You speak too fast, Ofelia."

"The Ferguson's, the family who bought the home? They told

me about your little escapade—you are so lucky they called me and not the police."

"It's good to hear from you. I miss you. You should call more often," Gian says.

"Dad, listen to me. Do. Not. Go. Back. There. Okay? I know you weren't 'in the area' and it is so, so not okay that you talked their little girl into letting you in. It's creepy. You're so lucky I work with Zabine, or you would be in serious trouble."

"I tried calling you yesterday, you didn't answer."

"Seriously dad, don't play dumb, okay? Just...Look, I have to get back to work. Can you please not break and enter?"

"You should come visit. See where I'm living. I have an orchid now."

"I have to go. I'll call you later, please just stay out of trouble."

"It's beautiful, not like having a garden, of course, but it's something," he says, but she's already hung up.

~ o ~

Darcy knocks on the door of the flat opposite hers, number 203. Michelle opens it a crack and for a moment Darcy has a sense of Deja Vu as she remembers taking the basket to Mr. Verdi. All these people living so close together, totally reluctant to let anyone have even the slightest glimpse into their lives. Michelle's probably just woken up, of course. It's early, which would account for her tangled hair, but to Darcy she has the look of someone hiding more than just bed head.

"Sorry to bother you. Some of your post ended up in our box." Darcy holds out the envelope Felicity has failed to bring over for three days. Darcy discovered it that morning, tucked under a stack of papers building up on the coffee table since school began again.

"It's probably not important anyway," Felicity said, dismissively, when Darcy showed it to her.

"Dude, it's a bill. Look at it." Darcy held it up to demonstrate the telltale signs of being an important piece of post. This was still lost on Felicity, who told Darcy, if she thought it was so important, that she could take it to them.

Michelle opens the door a bit more so she can take the envelope, her hair slipping to the side.

"Thank you," Michelle says, before pushing the door shut, inches from Darcy's face. Darcy has a class to get to, but she hesitates. The cut above Michelle's eye, and the bruising on her cheek, was unmistakable in the moment before she shut the door.

The conundrum is if Darcy should knock again. She considers the early hour — it's not even eight yet. She has no idea what the situation is, regardless of her best guess, and knows she could risk making things worse. But then, maybe by not knocking things would get worse anyway? It's like that famous story of the woman being murdered in broad daylight in New York. Everyone thought someone else would call the police so nobody did. No wonder people resort to splitting, thinks Darcy — it's all an attempt to avoid how bloody complicated life is.

Thankfully Franklin emerges from their flat just then, asking her what's she doing.

"Uh, contemplating a moral dilemma."

"You look like a stalker. Stalking is morally wrong. No dilemma. Don't do it."

Darcy rolls her eyes, shifting her rucksack to keep it from slipping down her shoulder.

"Did you return their post?" Franklin asks, his back to her as he locks the door.

"Yeah. I did. But..." Darcy crosses the hall to stand near him and in a hushed voice she says, "I think her boyfriend hits her."

Franklin's eyebrows shoot up into his shaggy hairline.

"She had a bruise on her cheek when I saw her a few weeks ago, and this morning she has a proper black eye."

"Uh huh." Franklin begins walking towards the lift, Darcy trailing along behind him, reluctantly.

"Doesn't that concern you?" she asks.

"Not particularly," Franklin says, as he presses the lift button.

"Felicity got a black eye last year when she was texting and walking, and she hit that pole. She sprained her ankle the next month when she wore those ridiculous shoes and got super drunk. She currently has a burn on her hand from reaching over the boiling kettle for a mug."

"Yeah, but all those things are, like, obvious accidents," Darcy says.

"Yeah, and maybe that woman has had some obvious accidents. There are a lot of ways to get bruise or cut. It doesn't have to mean her boyfriend did it. Or maybe she hit him, and he had to hit her in self-defence." Franklin shrugs. "No need to jump to conclusions."

The lift opens, and they step on, but Darcy is hesitant, keeping one foot out to block the door.

"Okay. Fair enough. But what if he is hitting her and no one has asked and if they did it could make a huge difference?"

"Like how?"

Darcy gives Franklin her best baffled expression. "How? Well like, she could go to a shelter or something."

"Darcy, do you seriously think that if you ask her if she's being abused and if she's actually honest about it if she is, that it will be a matter of her just up and leaving like that?" The door starts to beep, and Franklin pulls her on, letting it close.

"Okay. It sounds dumb when you put it that way," says Darcy. And then, after a moment of thought, she adds, "But she could seriously need some help and if someone just offered…"

"Fine. Then offer some help if you're so worried."

The lift opens on the ground floor and Darcy wants to defiantly press the button and go back up. But she knows she won't. Franklin has made her doubtful, despite herself. She concedes that she doesn't know the details of the situation.

"Exactly. You don't want to make an ass of yourself." Franklin ruffles her hair affectionately.

~ o ~

Jacob's voice sounds concerned, "Is this woman paying you, though, ma?"

"Of course not! I wouldn't accept it if she tried," Hester does love her son, and looks forward to their weekly phone call, but she dislikes when he speaks to her as though she were a naive child.

"It's just a big drain on you. I wouldn't want to think of you being taken advantage of."

"Darling, I'll decide what's a drain on me, thank you very much. Malik is a delightful little boy. You're always worried about me being lonely? Well, now I'm not lonely. It's an absolute joy to spend my day with him, and Namisha, bless her, is a kind and wonderful woman. I enjoy her company.

"Now, enough about me and my boring life, how are your studies? How are you doing?"

"I'm fine. Look, if you ever feel too tired just tell her you can't do it, right?"

Hester does her best not to sound cross. "I do know how to look after myself, love. I was doing it for years before you came along."

"I just want to make sure you're being careful, that's all. It's hard when I'm not there to look out for you."

"Oh Jacob, look out for me over something practical—like a tradesman trying to get my money for installing dodgy antennae or something like that. You hear all sorts about people selling products to old ladies, never delivering the goods and taking all the money. I assure you that a young mother and baby are not scheming anything nearly so heinous.

"I'd like you to meet them when you come down next, I know it will put your mind at ease. You'll see how lovely they are."

"Okay, fine. I am looking into when I can come down, but I can't promise anything."

"Oh don't you fret, darling. Just go ahead and save your money. I'll see you at Christmas anyway." She pauses and then asks, "So, have you found a new roommate?"

"Uh... no. No, I'm... enjoying having the space to myself for a bit."

"You don't need any help making the rent do you?"

"No ma, don't worry."

"Well, there you go then. If I'm not allowed to worry about you, you certainly aren't allowed to worry about me. It's only fair."

She's pleased to hear him laugh and tells him as much. They natter on a bit longer, not about anything in particular, until he says he has to go. As she disconnects from the call, she can't help noticing the distinctive lack of sadness she used to feel so very acutely every time they said goodbye in the past. She still misses him, of course. He's the light of her life—but he's no longer the only other person in it.

The flat is dark, the curtains are drawn, and all the lights are switched off. Chelle lays on the sofa, feeling as though she's been hit by a truck. She's actually been hit by a tin. It fell from the top shelf of the cupboard as she was reaching for a box of muesli first thing that morning, striking her on the eyebrow right above the eye. As with any head wound, the blood was out of proportion to the size of the cut, so when Darren emerged from the bedroom and saw her, he was instantly upset.

"What the Hell happened, Chelle!"

She got him to calm down, remarking on what a big baby he was and that, as the one with the head wound, he should be calming her down. Together they went to the bathroom to inspect it and after wiping the blood away, they both agreed it wasn't so deep and certainly didn't need stitches. Of course, by then her eye was already swelling up, and the pain was enough to make her feel quite sick. Darren told her to wait in the bathroom while he got some ice but she followed him in the kitchen anyway, as looking at it in the mirror was making her feel much worse.

Darren made her sit on the sofa, pressing a bag of frozen peas wrapped in a towel to her forehead. He got her a cup of tea and then, apologetically, said he had to go, or he'd be late for work. He also apologised for being such a dick the night before and promised he'd call her when he was on his lunch break, to make sure she was okay. "You call me, though, if you feel any worse. And take something for the pain. You're going to have one Hell of a headache." He kissed her on the forehead, above her other eye, and left for work.

Darren wasn't gone long when the American girl from across the hall came over with the post. Chelle couldn't remember her name. She looked like a lesbian, Darren said. Chelle thought she was quite striking. Her dark hair and dark brown eyes were startling against her pale skin. She was pretty sure she was one of those mixed kids. And she was just a kid, definitely. No more than nineteen, maybe.

As soon as the girl had gone, Chelle rang up her manager, to tell him she was concussed and wouldn't be in. He was surprisingly concerned and told her to go to A&E if she kept feeling ill.

She had a quick fag on the balcony before returning to the couch, where she's been asleep for maybe an hour. Her throat is sore now, and her chest feels thick and heavy. She coughs to try and get it moving, which sends a pounding pain up into her forehead. Every time she swallows it feels like there are razor blades in her throat.

Chelle gets up and shuffles through the bedroom into the bathroom. Her head is throbbing as she inspects herself in the mirror. Her eye is almost swollen shut. She runs a bath, the steam from the water setting off a coughing fit. Checking the time she remembers what Darren said about ringing at noon. It's nearly eleven so she goes back into the living room to grab her phone.

There's a text from Tim, asking if she's around and would like to chat. She taps out a quick reply, telling him she's not well, and hits send.

Immersing herself in the hot water of the now full tub, Chelle lets out a deep sigh, which almost immediately turns into a cough. It's like the universe doesn't want her to get pregnant, she thinks. All she wants is to sleep.

~ o ~

As Namisha lets herself into her flat Malik runs to greet her, wrapping his chubby arms around her legs. "Ma!"

"Hello, little man." She scoops him up under the arms, swinging him high into the air before settling him on her hip. His vocabulary has blossomed, and 'ma' has been his greeting every morning when he wakes up and when she gets home on the days she works. She loves the sound of his voice as he tries new words out, but 'ma' is unquestionably her favourite.

Hester was sitting in one of the kitchen chairs, but she gets up to put on the kettle almost immediately when Namisha comes through the door. This has become routine for the two of them. Namisha gets home, and Hester stays for an extra twenty minutes or so, making them each a cup of tea before they settle in to chat about their days. Today Hester and Malik did finger painting. Hester shows her the bumpy sheets laid out on the counter to dry. Namisha makes appropriate noises to indicate how impressed she is with Malik's handiwork, as he giggles and wiggles in her arms.

Namisha sets him down and stretches out on the sofa, resting her head against one arm. She lets out a deep sigh, grateful to be lying down.

"Was it a rough day, then?" Hester asks.

"Oh no," she says. "Not rough. Just long. And too nice to be cooped up inside. I also had a run-in with an elderly gentleman in the lobby as I came in—literally. He ran into me."

"He wasn't wearing a tweed cap was he?"

Namisha furrows her brow. "I think he was, yes. Why?"

"He's in two-oh-five. An Italian gentleman, my age or near enough?" Hester brings Namisha her mug of tea, which she sits up to take. "He's a tough nut to crack, certainly. I see him out and about sometimes, he's always scowling."

"He moved in last month, didn't he?"

"About then, yes," Hester says. She's sits back down in the kitchen, and Malik crawls over, trying to climb into her broad lap. Namisha watches as the elderly woman lifts up her son, pulling him in for a squeeze. He giggles and kicks his feet, and she thinks of her parents, especially her mother, who would be so happy to know her grandson.

Her life has changed so much since the day they turned her away—her father turned her away. There was so much sadness for a time, or perhaps dullness is a better word for it, she thinks. As she watches Hester bouncing Malik on her knee, Namisha realises, even if things aren't perfect, that she's actually happy.

~ o ~

The water cascades down over Tim's head as he stands in the shower. He closes his eyes, letting it cover his face, the warmth of it a familiar comfort. The feeling in his chest is like a bruise. When it was fresh the slightest movement caused him immense pain, but now it's just tender, sensitive only if prodded. Tim imagines if he could look at it, the bruise would be turning sort of yellow now. He's trying not to look at it, though.

He spent the day orienting himself to the tasks required of him in his new contract. Normally he works from home, but the client insisted he come into their office. He took a bus and then the tube into Vauxhall to sit in a cramped office space as a project manager, who knows very little about the kind of thing Tim does, went over the specs of the job. It's simple work—adding a few plug-ins to a WordPress site—but as soon as Tim sat down to it, the work was genuinely the only thing on his mind. The relief of this was immense and he felt disappointed when his work day ended and he had to make the long journey back home.

It's the voicemail that's making it difficult for him to ignore the bruise, as he stretches his neck first to one side and then the other, the hot droplets of water soaking his sore muscles. Tim spotted it as he waited for the bus, it having probably come in when he was underground. The number was withheld and, unthinkingly, he plugged his headphones into the phone and pressed play.

Rachael's voice came through, simultaneously comforting and unwelcome. He swore, drawing attention to himself from an older woman standing nearby. He'd smiled at her, apologetically, fumbling to delete the message. But it was too late, as he'd heard most of it.

"Look, I know I'm the last person you think you want to talk to right now, and I apologise for what happened last time in that I probably should have asked to meet somewhere more private, but I knew you wouldn't have agreed to that. But I don't apologise for what I said. I know you loved…love him. I do, but Jack was manipulative. I just want what's best for you…"

Hot tears mix with the water running down his face, as Tim leans forward, resting his forehead on the tile wall.

In a fit of something he couldn't really explain, he'd sent a text to Chelle. He's never been particularly gregarious, preferring computers to people. He made a few friends in Uni, but after graduating everyone scattered, across the UK or Europe. In the last few years, the friends he'd had were mostly Jack's. They'd liked Tim well enough but he'd never been really close with anyone… besides Rachael.

When Chelle responded almost right away to say she wasn't well, he felt deflated. He'd decided to take a few sleeping pills, hop in the shower and then go to bed. It was early but when he was sleeping he was dreaming and in his dreams Jack still loved him, and that was all that mattered.

~ o ~

Hester gathers up little Jacob in her arms, breathing deeply of his baby smell. Next to her Malik is babbling away, sitting in the grass. She looks around at the lake, the water reflecting the bright sun. She sets Jacob down, and he crawls over to where Malik sits. Her lovely little boys, naked in the sun, Jacob's skin a rich sepia, so much darker than she'd expected, and Malik, a light russet with olive undertones.

They both look behind them, towards the rolling hills, and Hester follows their gaze. Namisha is walking over the pebbled beach of the lakeshore, a beautiful sari wrapped around her—all gold and red. She's far away though and doesn't appear to be getting nearer. She's calling, her voice hard to hear. And then there's the sound of thunder. Hester looks to the lake, wondering if there's a storm coming, but the sound is too repetitive now, not like thunder at all. The scene wavers, rippling. She looks up and sees someone with a hammer, a shadowy figure beating on the sky.

Hester opens her eyes to the darkness of her bedroom, the lake still glimmering in her mind's eye. The sound, the regular pounding, hasn't stopped. There's a voice, raised in anger, but muffled. It takes Hester a moment to realise she's been dreaming. She struggles to turn on her bedside lamp. The glowing red numbers on her clock radio indicate it's a little past four in the morning.

She moves as quickly as her aching joints will allow, pulling on her dressing gown and carefully picking her way past furniture in the dark sitting room to get to the front door. She can't make out specific words, but someone is definitely yelling. She peers through the peephole to see what all the ruckus is about.

A man bangs his fist against Namisha's door, which is open a crack and shakes under his attack. He's hard to make out, but Hester notes his leather jacket, shoulder-length brown hair, and that he's white. He seems to be trying to wedge his foot into the bottom of the door. Hester needs only the briefest moment to take this in before she grabs a walking stick and unlocks her door. She lets out a loud whoop as she strides across the hall, hitting the intruder across the shoulders. The man whips his arm out, his quick movement taking her by surprise. She stumbles backwards, a sharp pain in her ankle causing her leg to fold beneath her.

Hester's blow, though not damaging, gives Namisha the opportunity to shut the door. The intruder begins to kick it. "You cow! I know you know where he is! Tell me where he is!"

Almost simultaneously the doors on either side of Namisha's flat fly open. The young man from number 201 looks first at the man and then at Hester, who is trying to pull herself back towards her still open door. He moves over to her, grabbing her stick from where it fell, and takes her hand.

The man from 203 adopts a different approach. He clamps his hands down on the shoulders of the intruder, who is, by comparison, incredibly short. The intruder swings wildly, swearing and trying to hit his captor, who, holding the lapel of his leather jacket in one hand, effortlessly lifts him off the floor.

"Fuck. Right. Off." Hester flinches and the young man squeezes her hand quite tightly, as their neighbour punches the man, knocking him out cold with a single hit.

For a moment the hallway grows quiet.

The man from 203 releases his grip, letting the unconscious man slump to the floor. He turns to Hester. "You okay?"

She nods, and so does the young man kneeling next to her, although from the way he's breathing she suspects he's not okay at all. Hester pats his hand, which has an almost painful grip on her own. He flinches before giving her a weak smile and finally letting go.

The door of 202 opens a crack, the chain still on, and Namisha looks out.

"You okay?" The man from 203 asks again. Namisha nods and Hester tries her best to meet her eye, to communicate that she's there for the young woman. She's also trying not to think about the incredible pain in her foot and ankle.

"Baby, is everything okay?" All heads turn and Hester sees the young woman from 203 peering out of her flat. Her hair is a bird's nest mess, her eyes wide and gleaming against pale skin, which looks all the paler for the black eye she's sporting.

As if to complete the scene, Darcy pops her head out of 206 and she too asks if everything is okay.

~ o ~

That morning's rude awakening several hours before she needed to be up, combined with the drone of this particular lecturer, is a perfect sedative for Darcy. She rubs her eyes, blinking them rapidly in an attempt to wake herself up a bit more.

She's had several cups of coffee, but the effect has just been a racing heart, rather than an antidote to fatigue.

Felicity is the one who woke Darcy. Franklin sleeps like it's going out of style—so he hadn't heard a thing. Although Darcy hadn't either until Felicity was there, shaking her awake, telling her something was going on and that she was scared.

"You? You're scared?" But then Darcy heard the bellowing too, someone shouting about money and swearing. Darcy pulled on some clothes and went to the front door, where Felicity was looking through the peephole. The angle was wrong, though, they couldn't see a thing. In hushed whispers, they discussed what to do. Darcy basically drew the short straw, although by then the pounding and yelling had stopped, so she didn't mind being the one to poke her head out to investigate.

It was all pretty surreal from then on, like something out of a movie or a soap opera. The police and an ambulance were called, by Chelle's boyfriend, Darren, who was nicer than Darcy had expected. Chelle herself disappeared back into her flat to lie down. Darren said she'd had an accident the day before and had also come down with something, that she was a real wreck, and neither of them had been sleeping well when the noise started.

There was speculation on how the guy had gotten in. When the police arrived everyone was asked to give a statement, except for Hester, who had been taken away by ambulance before the cops got there.

Darcy had been so groggy from the combination of adrenalin and a lack of sleep that she found it difficult to answer anything they asked. Felicity knew more anyway, or at the very least had heard more of the commotion than Darcy. Their answers mostly matched when it came to how much they knew about Namisha. No, they didn't really know her well. They weren't aware that she'd been living with a known drug dealer. Darcy pointed out that he'd not been there for some time anyway. "I've not seen him in months. Seriously. He's just not been there."

"Really?" Felicity was doubtful.

"Yeah—didn't you notice that? She's been on her own for ages."

The officer who took their statement thanked them, before crossing over to where her colleague was questioning Tim. A third officer had already collected the intruder, who regained consciousness but was considerably subdued when he was led away. Darcy hoped that Darren didn't get into any trouble for punching the guy. As far as she was concerned, Darren was a total hero.

Once they were back in the flat Darcy wanted to get more sleep, but it was nearly six, and she'd only have a half hour, if that. Besides, Felicity was in a total flap. She kept asking how someone like that could get in and what they should do to protect themselves. Darcy found herself in the annoying position of having to talk her down. When Franklin woke up they went through the whole thing again, telling him all the details, Darcy doing her best to temper the exaggerated version coming from Felicity. And then it had been time for her to get ready to go, or she'd be late.

So here Darcy is, barely able to keep her head up. She's doing her best to take notes because she knows this particular lecture is covering something that will account for 40% of their final mark, but all she wants is to crawl into the cosy nest that is her bed.

~ o ~

"So, you're all settled in then?" The care worker sits on the sofa across from Gian, a clipboard in her hand. He wonders about the clipboard as it always seems to have lined paper on it and yet she never writes anything down.

"You never write anything," he tells her.

"Sorry?"

He points to the clipboard. "You bring it every time but don't write on it. Why have it?"

As if he hasn't spoken she asks him, louder this time, how he's finding the flat.

"It's dangerous," he tells her. "Some junkie was here yesterday. He killed the old lady next door."

She speaks to him like he's an infant, telling him that simply isn't true, as if she was the one who was here when it happened and not him. He saw the old woman, lying on the floor, saw the paramedics come up and lay her out on a stretcher. Then there were the police, asking questions, as if he would associate with such people. He'd given them an earful about disturbing an old man—an innocent old man.

One of the officers, a woman, explained about a known drug dealer living there. He told her he wasn't surprised, had suspected them all along. Then there had been more questions—why he'd suspected it, who he was referring to when he said 'them', was the wife part of it as well?

"What wife?"

"You said 'them' sir, that implies more than one person."

"Well, I don't know. Maybe it's just that one, the one who dresses like a boy."

"Who are you referring to, sir?"

At that point her partner had stepped in, saying something else. Gian waved his hands at them both. "I keep telling you, I don't know anything! I'm an old man who just wants his rest. I didn't even want to move here!"

He shut the door on them, which the care worker remarked on when she first arrived. He guesses this is the sole reason for her visit.

"I'm not a child."

"Of course not, Mr. Verdi. No one is saying you are. It's just, the police were concerned that you might have information that could help them in their investigation."

"I'm not a criminal!" He knows he's getting worked up, but his whole day has been ruined. It all happened so early. He missed his walk, his espresso and warm roll. He'd not even made his coffee when it all started. And then the police took up more of his time. He'd only just gotten dressed, finally had a cup of coffee, when the care worker appeared at the door.

"I want to talk to my daughter."

"Of course you do. Of course. I'm sure you're very shaken up." She leans forward, patting his knee. He moves to brush her hand away, but she's already removed it, slipping the clipboard into her oversized handbag, pulling it up over her shoulder. "I'll leave you be then. Let you ring her. I'll be in touch again in a few weeks."

And like that, he's alone again.

T im looks straight ahead, concentrating on the road as he makes his way down Tooting High Street. Next to him Namisha is quiet, her head resting on the window. He thinks she's fallen asleep.

He offered to give her a lift to the hospital using his member-ship in a car share. Together they figured out how to dismantle Malik's pram, which separated so it could be used as a car seat, and installed it in the back.

The last time Tim has been to a hospital was a trip to the A&E, a little over a year ago. He'd had been out in the garden, on the roof of the tiny shed where Jack kept his gardening tools. He was stapling down some new tar paper covering when he lost his footing and fell. It hadn't been far, but he hit his elbow and his knee pretty hard when he landed. Afterwards, Tim couldn't straighten his arm, and Jack insisted they go to the hospital.

The wait was long, since it wasn't a critical injury. Jack started off quite sweet but after forty minutes he began to complain about the people around them, remarking on how many 'chavs' ended up in A&E. He'd look at Tim, expecting him to laugh, as he made mean comments—and all Tim could think was that the pain in his elbow wasn't nearly so bad as the pain of the person he loved spouting such cruel things. Tim told Jack he'd much rather be there alone if Jack was just going to make fun of people. Jack had gone quiet, but not, Tim thought, because he felt sorry for what he'd been saying. It's a memory that stings, but not in the same way as Tim's broken heart.

When Tim and Namisha arrive at the hospital Malik begins to kick up a fuss. He squeezes his hands into little fists and refuses to hold still as Namisha attempts to undo the clip on his seat, making hush-hush noises at the same time. Malik's face screws up in anger, his voice rising to a shriek as he kicks his feet.

Namisha looks around the crowded parking lot before cooing to Malik, to get him to calm down. "Come on, baby boy. I know you're tired, darling."

She squeezes her eyes shut, and Tim sees she's at the end of what she can deal with. He puts a hand on her shoulder, gently pulling her to her feet so he can take her place. Slipping down to his knees so he's eye level with Malik he says, "You like sitting there?"

Malik stares at him, his chin quivering, hands still bunched into fists. He nods once, and a single tear runs down his cheek, stopping at his chin. Tim wipes it away. "That's cool. It's a nice seat. Look, if you want to sit there, you can. Just hold very still."

Tim fiddles with the seatbelt and in one swift movement pulls the entire thing out of the car.

"Thank you," Namisha says.

Tim balances the seat on his hip. "This isn't so bad. I can carry him up."

"No, I mean... for this. For everything. For yesterday, the ride, for being here." Her expression is so earnest Tim has to look away.

"Hey." Tim feels his face flush red, his cheeks hot. "You've had a shit day. A few shit days. It's the least I can do."

~ o ~

In the lift, a woman wearing teal scrubs, about fifty, with a sensible short haircut and white freckled skin, smiles at Tim and Namisha. "You have a beautiful family," she says.

Tim grins at the woman, but Namisha can only manage a small, lopsided smile in return. She's unbelievably tired, too tired to correct the woman, and all too aware that Malik should be napping, although he seems calm enough now, sat on his throne in Tim's arms.

They find Hester in an open area of the wing she's in, and Namisha swiftly crosses to her. As they hug, Namisha can't help thinking the old woman is offering her comfort, despite Hester being the one in hospital. She's reluctant to pull away, but Malik is squealing for her, saying 'auntie'.

"Oh, I've been so naughty." Hester giggles, reaching out to take Malik from Tim. "I told them he was my grandson. I knew they'd let you up if I did that."

"He misses you," Namisha says.

Hester turns to Tim, her smile broad and bright. "And you! You're my saviour. Bless you, dear boy."

Namisha collects Malik up in her arms as Hester motions for Tim to come closer so she can take his hand. "You, young man, are a gem. A real gem! I want Jacob to meet you, all three of you! It would have been nicer under better circumstances, but here we are.

"He's gone to get me a shawl, but he should be back soon. Silly love, I told him an extra blanket from the nurses would be fine, but he insisted, properly insisted, that I have something nice that I could keep. He's always buying me little things like that. It's sweet."

Namisha's heart flutters when Hester's son appears a moment

later, carrying a bag from Marks & Spencer. He's tall, his skin a bit lighter than his mother's but still a rich brown. He has a short neatly trimmed beard and hair. Hester does the round of introductions and Jacob shakes both her and Tim's hands, very formally. Namisha bows her head, surprised at how intimidated she feels. She's heard so much about Jacob, but it's very different to meet the actual person. She wrestles with overwhelming guilt, certain he blames her for what happened. And why wouldn't he? If Hester hadn't come into their life the way she had, would she have been so protective?

Namisha's still trying to piece it all together. She didn't know the man who came around, although his face was familiar. Chris had any number of 'guy friends' and rarely put in the effort to introduce her to them. She'd not been bothered, though. That's how boys were. They didn't see the importance of giving names, and she wasn't that interested in knowing Chris' friends anyway. But he'd not been a friend, apparently. The police referred to him as one of Chris' 'business associates'.

Namisha realises she's barely there in the hospital, her mind is so foggy with fatigue. Hester is saying how wonderful it was for them to come visit her, how seeing so many friendly faces is good for her. Tim is still standing by her bed, looking to Namisha as if he feels out of place.

"You're only supposed to have two visitors at a time, Ma," Jacob says, leaning in to kiss Hester on the temple.

Namisha apologises. "We really should be going. Malik is usually down for a nap right now."

"Nonsense! It's perfectly okay for you to stay a little longer. He's happy as Larry here." Hester bounces Malik in her hands, and he does seem content, but Namisha sees how Jacob looks at her, his jaw tight.

"I know. But I need to get him back into his routine, and you really should be getting rest." Namisha collects Malik into her arms and is grateful when Hester nods.

"Of course, dear. Of course. It's so important to give little ones stability. And big ones too." She winks at Namisha. "I'll be home soon enough. You can bring him around to visit then."

~ o ~

The cabbie mumbles about Gian being a 'cheap bugger' before speeding off towards central London and better fares. Gian pockets the two coins change on the nine pounds seventy pence fare he paid ten pounds for. He gave up on public transport and gone for the cab due to a rowdy group of teenagers on the bus and a cancelled train—the final connection meant to get him to his daughter's house.

He stands outside the semi-detached, two-storey building. He's only been here once before, on the day of Bella's funeral, but not inside. His daughter had been driving him around that day—his license had been revoked a few months prior—and she needed to run in for a few things between the service and the reception. She told him to wait in the car, locking the doors as she got out, as if he was a naughty child. Very little about the house has changed since then. It has little white window boxes and newly pointed bricks. The window boxes are full of lumpy dirt and stained with pigeon excrement, and the painted trim is tired and weather damaged.

Gian steps cautiously up the cracked pavement, narrowly avoiding tripping over a particularly uneven bit. Lifting the heavy brass knocker, he takes in the cracked, grey paint on the front door. It's peeling away to revealing layers of other colours beneath.

Ofelia opens the door, an expectant look on her face which immediately changes to a scowl. She's wearing a dark suit, dress trousers and a blazer done up over a white blouse. Her hair is pulled up into a bun, her makeup impeccable, just like her mother. "What are you doing here?"

"Is that any way to greet your father?" He puts his arms out. She remains where she is, leaning against the edge of the door frame, her own arms crossed.

"We should go in, it's chilly," Gian says.

"Why are you here?"

"Does a father need a reason to come see his favourite daughter?"

"I'm your only daughter and hardly a favourite. I said I'd call you. You can't just come around unannounced."

"There was an accident, an intruder where I'm living now. I had to talk to the police."

She rolls her eyes. "What's this about?"

"Please, may I come in?" He shivers, pulling his wool coat tightly around his shoulders. She taps one stockinged foot on the door frame, pursing her lips at him. Finally, she steps back, swinging the door wide. Turning, she walks down the hall. "Shut the door behind you."

He follows her in, unwinding his scarf and unbuttoning his coat as he walks down the tiny hall. It leads past a small sitting room into a dining room with large glass doors facing out to the back garden. There is also a kitchen, not more than a few metres square, off to the left. Gian sees it's full of gleaming appliances. There is no clutter anywhere he looks, nothing is left out.

He takes off his tweed cap, holding both it and his scarf in clenched fists. "I miss you. You never call. I thought it would be a pleasant surprise if I came to you. I know how busy you are with your work..."

Ofelia lets out a long puff of air through her nose, like a snorting bull, "You never appreciated that before."

"May I have a cup of tea? I've been travelling for over an hour."

Her jaw remains clenched. "Fine. One cup of tea."

He smiles graciously, but she's already turned away. He pulls out one of the chairs, which creaks as he sits down.

"You never drank tea before," she says from the kitchen.

He looks around himself. The inside of the house is in significant contrast to the outside. The hardwood floor is impeccably clean, the table in the dining room old polished wood surrounded with a set of antique chairs. There's a sideboard with a glass vase on it.

"I said," Ofelia comes to the doorway of the kitchen, "you never drank tea before."

"I still don't. I remember you never liked making coffee."

"I didn't like," she enunciates her words carefully, each one a sharp punctuation, "that you felt entitled to having mum and I wait on you hand and foot."

"Your mother loved me. We loved each other."

Her response to this is to raise a single, dark eyebrow in one sharp motion.

"I miss her." He looks away.

"So do I," Ofelia snaps, before turning back into the kitchen. Gian puts his hat and scarf on the table, running his hand along its uneven surface. They had one very like it in the family home. He wonders if Ofelia remembers, if that's why she bought this. He recognises the bookshelf in the corner, which looks just as it did when it belonged to Bella. The shelves are full of her cookbooks, which he knows are full of her looping handwriting—notes on recipes that have long since been forgotten, uncooked for years.

Ofelia reappears carrying two steaming mugs, one of which she sets down in front of Gian. The rich, dark aroma of coffee floats up. "You made coffee."

"I was making one for myself when you knocked."

"It's the anniversary today." He looks at her. Her eyes, a dark blue-grey just like Bella's, remain hard. "We're family. We should be together on such a day."

"We were never much of a family."

"You blame me."

"Of course I blame you. Who else is there? You were the one who always pushed us, pushed everyone to be better than they were, better than anyone could possibly be.

"Why do you think he started using? It was the pressure of living up to your shitty expectations. That pressure kept mum awake at night, cleaning up after you, carrying on after you, until she had a heart attack. It's a wonder I'm still alive."

Gian winces, Ofelia's words prodding his unspoken guilt and shame. He isn't sure why he came, what he expected, and yet he's not surprised. Standing up, Gian collects his hat and scarf.

He looks at her, tears in his eyes.

"I'm sorry," he says. And Gian walks out, leaving his coffee untouched.

~ o ~

Darren storms about the flat, slamming cupboards and throwing away packaging from last night's tea. Chelle winces from where she's sitting out on the balcony. She's having a fag. Her throat is still sore, but she finds the smoke loosens up her chest a bit.

Cheering Darren up had been a total failure. She told him he'd done a good thing, had probably stopped things from getting so much worse.

"Fucking trash. I can't stand trash like that. I hate how trash like that had me carted down to the police!" he'd shouted.

"Don't yell at me!" She tried calming him down, assuring him it was okay, even though he'd had to miss work. "You boss will understand. You aren't to blame, the police even said. You probably kept things from getting much worse."

But Darren had just been all dramatic, going on about losing his job. She tried pointing out that they wouldn't even find out— he could just say he was sick. It was Friday evening, so he'd easily be recovered by a Monday, no one would doubt him.

When she said that, Darren held up his split knuckles. "How do you figure these will be healed by Monday, then?"

That was when she got fed up and came out here, onto the balcony. Darren isn't calming down, though, so after a bit she stubs out her smoke, goes back inside and grabs her coat. He snaps at her as she opens the front door, "Where are you going?"

"Out."

"You're still sick!"

"Yeah, well sticking around with you in this mood isn't going to make me feel any better."

She knows she isn't really helping, as she slams the door, but she's just too tired. He's acting like a big baby. So sensitive and precious, making a big deal out of nothing.

She stops at the pub just up the road from the flats. It's a dingy place with sticky floors and a permeating smell of spilled alcohol. It takes a moment for her eyes to adjust to the dim space. She's never really been a drinker, unlike Darren. She's no taste for beer or wine, really. Sugary alcopops make her feel sick and hard liquor makes her cough. She's deciding on what to order when a voice to her left makes her jump.

"Did he do that to you?"

Chelle hadn't noticed Darcy standing just around the corner of the bar. The younger woman leans forward, a pint of beer in her hand. "Sorry Michelle, I didn't mean to startle you."

Chelle touches a finger to the edge of her bruised eye, confused that Darcy thinks the man from that morning got anywhere near her. "No. He didn't lay a hand on me."

Darcy arches an eyebrow at her, disbelieving.

"It's not really any of your business, is it?" Chelle snaps.

"Hey—no offence meant. I just thought I should ask, but if you say your boyfriend didn't hit you, then I believe you. You can stand up for yourself, clearly."

Chelle rolls her eyes. "Oh, what? Darren? No, this was a tin. It fell out of the cupboard when I was trying to put stuff away."

"Oh gawd, that's so embarrassing. One of those stupid things that really hurts but damages your pride more, right?"

Darcy offers to buy her a drink. Chelle had wanted to be alone, but the other woman is insistent. After a moment's hesitation, she gives in. "Fine. If you're buying, I'll have a whisky. And my name is Chelle, or, that's what I go by."

"Cool, Chelle. Happy to treat you." Darcy smiles and leans in to wave the bartender over.

~ o ~

It's just gone one in the morning when Darcy suggests that maybe they should head home. She'd realised pretty quickly that Chelle wasn't well—her voice squeezed and husky. She coughed up a storm after drinking the whisky and from then on Darcy insisted she drink only water, which Chelle did after another two glasses.

They've spent most of the night talking about Darren, or rather, talking about Chelle's frustrations with Darren. Picking it apart and putting it back together. Darcy tried to approach it like therapeutic practice, but she figures her lack of a formal qualification is further diminished by being intoxicated.

Darcy is surprised when Chelle insists they go outside so she can have a 'quick smoke', thinking it probably isn't the best idea. But at least Chelle has a smile on her face now, instead of that dark look when she'd first walked into the pub.

"You're brilliant. Really." Chelle puts her arm around Darcy's shoulders as they step out into the cool night air. It's refreshing and helps Darcy clear her head some.

Chelle babbles on about how helpful Darcy's been. "I've not had a proper chin-wag like that in ages. I needed that, y'know? Proper needed it."

She leans heavily on Darcy, causing them to stumble slightly. Darcy put out her other arm to help her regain her footing and Chelle leans in, her lips brushing Darcy's. Startled, Darcy jumps back and Chelle stumbles further, dropping to one knee and starting into coughing fit.

As she recovers she looks up, her eyes bright with tears, "I just thought..."

"Hey now." Darcy closes the space between them, reaching a hand out to help Chelle get to her feet. "Look. We had good fun tonight, and I can get you're probably feeling pretty confused and junk."

"I'm not confused." Chelle jerks her head away. "I just thought maybe we—maybe if I was with a girl."

Darcy laughs, but not unkindly. "Oh, Chelle. Look, there are three major problems with that idea. One, women can be just as confusing and manipulative and weird to other women, maybe more-so. Two, even if you think he's a total git sometimes, this would constitute cheating on Darren."

"It's not the same, though."

"Yes, Chelle, trust me. It is. Doesn't matter that I'm a woman, or that we're drunk. It's cheating, and it's wrong. You don't want that karmic energy on your plate. Trust me. And besides, from everything you've told me, Darren genuinely loves you. And you're obviously in love with him too."

"So what's the third reason then?"

The third reason. The reason that Darcy is here and not in Canada. She takes a deep breath, "I'm in love with someone."

~ o ~

Hester listens to the sounds coming from the kitchen, cupboard doors closing softly, the tap running, the crinkle of a plastic package being opened. Jacob has, as always, done everything he can to make her comfortable—washing her bedding before she got home and then settling her in bed, her ankle propped up under two soft cushions. He's made her a cup of tea and bought her a new shawl, which she pulls tightly around her shoulders. He also moved one of the kitchen chairs into the room, so visitors can sit by her bed.

He comes into the room now, a small plate in his hand. "Just a few biscuits, mum. I did some grocery shopping for you so you have lots of fruit and veg."

"Don't you fret, dear. I'll be sure to eat my five a day." Hester winks, taking two biscuits from the plate he's holding out to her. He sits down, and she watches him as he nibbles the remaining biscuit and sips his tea. There's a little stitch in his brow. She thinks of it as his worry stitch. He's done it since he was little. On his grown face, with dark stubble coming in, it makes him look so much older than he is.

She does all she can to reassure him, but he always frets, her little Jacob. She's not sure where he gets it from as she's never been one to worry. She supposes such seriousness helps him, though. Why he's so studious, why he does so well in medicine.

Not that she fools herself about the gravity of the situation. It could have been her hip and next time it might be. She's been unsteady on her feet for some time and apparently her old bones are getting brittle to have snapped from such a small stumble, but she just doesn't see the point in dwelling on 'what ifs'. She's just happy that Namisha and little Malik are safe, that no one else got hurt and that people still look out for each other.

She sets her now empty mug on her bedside table and pats the edge of the bed, by her hip, to indicate that Jacob should move closer. He sighs, putting his still half full mug and the now empty plate on the same table as he moves to sit next to her. "What is it, mum?"

Taking his hand, she traces tiny circles on his palm with the tips of her fingers. It's something she used to do for him as a little boy when he was upset or ill. The furrow in his brow loosens. She's always thought she'd live well into her eighties, a sort of gut feeling—but what one thinks and what might happen aren't always going to be the same. She doesn't believe it's her place to question or assume what might be in store for her, she just knows that she's been quiet for too long. They both have.

"I don't know what happened between you and Adam," she says. "If it was amicable or not, I mean. And I don't expect to know the details. But I want you to know, and this is all that really matters, I love you. I love all of you, and that means I love knowing about your life, as much as you're willing to share. I don't want you to feel like you can't tell me something because you think I won't understand. I'm not so foolish as you seem to think. Because I do understand. Probably more than you know."

As she speaks his eyes widen, his mouth parting in slight dismay. "There's a box in the sitting room, under my coffee table..."

At this, he flushes and looks down. "I know."

"You know?"

"I found the album months ago. I didn't look...Well, I mean, I did look at it, but not very closely. I realised it was...private."

"Oh love." Hester rests a hand on his cheek. "Love, it's not private from you. It's for you. I made it for you. I don't know what I planned for it, but I want you to have it—that's always been the intention. I knew you'd find it eventually. Once I'd gone, obviously you would. But bless you, my love, I don't want to wait. Secrets like these aren't worth keeping to the grave."

"I'm sorry I didn't tell you."

"Oh dear, I wouldn't have expected you to. It was my thing to tell you."

"No." He shakes his head. "Not about the box. About...about being gay."

At this Hester laughs. Smiling she says, "Oh love. You didn't have to. I've watched enough telly to know a thing or two about people. I figured it all out on my own. I could have spoken up at any time, but I thought I should just leave it until you were ready. Only, I know how these things can go. I don't suppose the church made it easy for you. God knows I couldn't stand some of them after a while. It's terrible how people use God to justify hating anybody.

"Now, tell me something: how much of that album did you read?"

C hris wasn't the kind of man Namisha imagined herself marrying—if she was honest, she hadn't actually considered getting married at all. She met him at a party one of her girlfriends encouraged her to sneak out to attend. He made her laugh. He was so different from all the brown boys she knew. She was twenty-two at the time, tired of her father's rules, of having to work in the family shop, of going to mosque and being lectured for only knowing English and not Hindi or Punjabi.

She didn't think of herself as rebellious, but when her father met Chris and instantly disapproved, she felt a thrill, a sense of control she'd never experienced before.

Her father would have been mortified to know she first had sex when she was seventeen. She'd done it with Damir, a guy her dad would have called 'a nice Indian boy'. Damir *was* nice—too nice. He was sweet, but it was with an almost obsessive kindness. All the focus was on her, no matter what they did together, and he seemed to think that sleeping together meant they were going to marry and have lots and lots of babies. Namisha didn't want that. She didn't want to be like her mum. She just wanted to have fun.

Perhaps this was the appeal, the difference that attracted her so much to Chris. He was kind and thoughtful, but he was also definitely fun. Namisha didn't feel like she was constantly being observed when she was with Chris. He cracked jokes and treated her much like he treated his guy friends. Chris also agreed that the way her father acted was oppressive, or in his words 'really old school', and was happy for her to move in with him.

When Namisha found out she was pregnant, she was surprisingly overjoyed. It was unexpected, an accident at the hands of laziness. They'd run out of condoms, he was 'pulling out'. She decided it was all part of a plan, meant to be. But it raised a question for her, one she would have to consider carefully: Was it better to have a child out of wedlock, or to be married to a white man?

She waited until her three-month scan to tell her parents. The three of them were in the sitting room, her parents on the loveseat, Namisha on a chair. She'd asked Chris not to come, deciding it was better to break the news on her own.

"Chris is excited. We're both excited. And we're getting married." She held out her hand so they could see the ring Chris had bought, like proof she had met and was in love with a good, decent man. She knew she was really trying to convince herself.

Namisha had been working since she was fifteen, first in her parent's shop—a place that sold knick-knacks and bric-a-brac—and then at a fast food chain. After finishing her A-levels, she started doing administrative work, which she enjoyed immensely. Chris, however, couldn't seem to hold down a job. He'd have one for a few weeks, and things would seem to be going alright, but then something would happen. He would tell her how the manager was an asshole or one of his co-workers had grassed him up, or sometimes he'd say it just wasn't 'his thing'. She'd come home to find him playing video games, although he insisted he'd been down to the job centre while she was working, that his CV was out there, and he was just waiting for things to come through.

Her father's words, as he banished her from his home, from ever seeing her siblings or her mother, were painful to hear. She didn't mind so much, that he insulted Chris. It wasn't even the insult to her. It was the punishment he was handing down to her unborn baby, his very own grandchild, whom he had never met.

When she got back to the flat she and Chris shared and told him what had happened, he was sympathetic. He pulled her in for a cuddle, told her not to worry. He'd find a job, he said, and support them all when the baby came. They went to the registry the following weekend. Namisha rang to invite her mum, but her father answered and wouldn't let them speak to each other.

Namisha worked right up until the day before she went into labour, and kept working part-time once Malik was born. Chris assured her he would be a good stay-at-home dad until he found a proper job. He was happy to look after the baby while she worked, happy to keep the flat in order. She tried not to let it get to her when she'd come home, and Chris was playing video games, the flat was a mess, and Malik propped up in some make-shift nest of pillows, usually in a dirty nappy. She thought, with time, Chris would start to pull his own weight. But then, just a month after he was born, Namisha came home to find Malik in his crib, crying and still wearing the same outfit and diaper she had put on him the night before. She was so tired, so entirely exhausted, mentally and physically. She was making mistakes at work from worrying about what was happening — or not happening — while she was away from the flat. HR said they were going to have to take disciplinary action soon. She didn't want to go through that and risk having it show on her CV and so, the next day, she gave notice. Then she went home and told Chris to go get a job. She said Chris had to hold up his end of this family and if he wasn't going to look after Malik during the day, then she would, and he could go work.

Chris had been humble about the whole thing. He said he would put in a real effort to get a job, that he had only been slacking off because he thought she wanted to focus on her career. And it didn't take him long, surprisingly. He spent a few days job hunting and suddenly, he had something doing 'odd jobs' for a contractor. He started coming home with cash. Some days there was a lot more than others, but Namisha didn't question it. She figured Chris was getting paid under the table. He gave her cash regularly, telling Namisha that he wanted to make sure she felt like she still had independence. She didn't go out, though, her time almost entirely occupied by Malik and keeping the flat clean. The bills went into a roll, a roll that got fatter and fatter.

It hadn't occurred to Namisha to be suspicious. She honestly hadn't known he was dealing drugs until the police questioned her, telling her that the man at her door had been trying to track her husband down because he owed someone quite a lot of money. She had been too busy planning her own escape, figuring out how she could get out of the strange life she'd managed to create for herself.

As Namisha lies on her bed, Malik curled up next to her, she smiles. She thinks of her new job, of Hester, of the ease she feels at this moment, lying next to her sleeping child. Rolling over, she rests a hand on his belly. He furrows his brow a little but doesn't wake and soon Namisha is sound asleep as well.

Things were different when Hester was a girl. Certainly, the importance of studying hard and getting grades was instilled in everyone, but it was only if you were a boy that you went on to a great and prominent career. If you were a girl you could go into nursing or an administration role, possibly even teaching, but the most important job expected of women was as a wife and a mother. So Hester married George, but by the time she was thirty she'd accepted that one or the other of them wasn't able to bear fruit.

George refused to get checked, and Hester suspected it was probably her with the problem anyway. They weren't interested in adoption and besides, it was the 60s. Things had moved on since she was a younger woman. With motherhood no longer in the cards, she went back to school to fill out her CV and soon she was working as an administrator at a law firm thanks to a connection through George.

When she reflects, Hester thinks it was when she was nearing her fortieth birthday that George started acting differently. He was sweet enough to her over the years, but George was never a particularly affectionate man—unless he wanted sex—so it was uncharacteristically kind of him to spontaneously bring home flowers or offer to do the washing up. He also began buying her little gifts like earrings, necklaces, a diamond ring. At first, she didn't think about it too much. Work kept her busy and on the weekends, when George was off golfing or on long business trips, Hester had her own activities to attend to, like her book club or helping out at church.

It was one of her friends, a woman she knew from George's office, who first mentioned his indiscretion. She was kind about it, asking Hester if George had mentioned the new secretary on staff. Hester rarely asked George about the comings and goings of his day and didn't know why it would be of interest to her. She said as much, and her friend touched her arm and raised her eyebrows in a knowing way.

After that, Hester began paying attention. It's incredible, she thought, how blind we can be. When we start looking at what is right in front of us, it's a wonder we were ever able to ignore it. There was the smell, unmistakably feminine, that she'd catch when he came home late. And the occasional stray hair, blue-black but too long to belong to either her or George. Granted, Hester did think that George had begun to get a bit sloppy when she came across a pair of ladies underwear in one of his pant legs while putting on a load of laundry. It was the day after he'd returned from a business trip. She considered confronting him with them but instead squirrelled them away in her sock drawer.

Hester wasn't surprised by her apathy towards the building evidence of his infidelity. Sex with George had often been a chore. In fact, she found it difficult to imagine him having an affair, as he had always been quite mechanical in bed, not the passionate type at all. She was relieved not to have the act required of her any longer, as she'd never enjoyed it much, and so Hester continued to play the ignorant wife, seeing no reason to do otherwise.

Just after her forty-sixth birthday, Jacob joined the firm. He was a young white man, about thirty-five, handsome and fit. All the women at the office seemed to swoon over him. Hester didn't pay him much mind, although she did agree that he was nice to look at. Clean shaven, Jacob wore tailored Savile Row waistcoats and trousers, his button down shirts always neatly pressed and adorned with charming cuff links. He greeted her every morning, asking how she was and sometimes bringing a piece of fruit, which he would put in a bowl she kept on her desk. He found out how she liked to take her tea and would bring her a cup, usually right when she was absolutely swamped and hadn't even managed a lunch break.

She appreciated these small kindnesses but thought little of them afterwards. It was a wonder their affair began at all but when it did it was instantly passionate.

She'd gone to make some photocopies and was walking back to her desk, passing Jacob's office on the way. He called out to her, and she paused, leaning in the doorway. "Yes?"

"Come in, shut the door. Have a seat."

She felt oddly nervous and unsure as to why. She was older than this man, and she had been at the firm for years. Jacob had no authority to discipline her, and she certainly wasn't expected to take orders from him. But she did as he asked, taking a seat in front of his mahogany desk.

"You've been here for quite a while, haven't you?"

"A few years now, yes," she said, with a nod.

"Ten."

"Yes, that may be true."

"Today is actually your tenth anniversary." He tapped a finger on the paper calendar covering most of his desk.

"How did you...?"

"I thought we should celebrate." He pulled out a bottle of champagne and two glasses from where he'd concealed them on the floor. Coming around to her, Jacob handed Hester a glass and placed the other on the desk. "You know, when you pop the cork, it's not meant to be with a bang but with a gentle sound, like a woman sighing."

He removed the wire and foil, gently easing the cork out so it released the softest sound of fizz from within. He poured her glass first and then his own. Lifting it in the air, he said, "A toast! To an immensely talented and intelligent woman."

They each sipped their Champagne and then Jacob leaned down and kissed her. Despite her belief in the importance of marriage, the sacredness of the union, it felt like the rightest thing in the world.

For the first time in her life, Hester understood the fascination people had with sex. Jacob was nothing like George. He was a courteous lover, who genuinely took an interest in her pleasure.

Because of her age, and her belief that she couldn't conceive anyway, they never used protection. Two months after their affair started, Hester began to feel bloated. After waking up queasy three days in a row, she went to the doctor.

George knew of course. Hester had not been intimate with him in months. But she had her trump card. She held up the lacy knickers she'd hidden away so long ago, and George said nothing.

She never blamed Jacob. He loved her, wanted nothing more than to be with her, but this complicated things. It was different then. People were adjusting to mixed couples, but it was still all too new. Jacob had his career to think about, and he couldn't risk a scandal. He also understood that she and George were at a stalemate. She couldn't support herself on her meagre salary, and George wanted to keep up appearances for his own career. So Hester and Jacob reluctantly parted ways, agreeing it was for the best.

For a few years, she and George raised baby Jacob as though he were their own. It was when Jacob began to walk and talk that George could no longer manage. The boy was not his and as Jacob began to grow George would always see the face of the man his wife had loved. She didn't blame him either, in the end.

That was the thing about people. Hester knew she could not expect that anyone should or could act differently than the best way they knew how.

Tim remembers, vividly, the moment he met Jack. He can still smell the sticky sweet scent of alcohol from the bar of the club they were in, the added musk of sweaty bodies, feel the throbbing bass of the dance music.

It was Tim's birthday, and he'd gone out with two former classmates who were getting ready to move to Australia and Canada, respectively. It was a night of celebration, of new jobs, of new adventures. Jack was wearing one of those LED shirts that flashes to the music. He stood at the bar, buying a shot for a friend and getting a bottle of water for himself. He overheard Tim telling the bartender that it was his birthday, asking if there was a discount, and offered to buy Tim a drink himself.

Tim could see, from the silver hair around his temples and the smile lines that crinkled the corner of his eyes, that Jack was older than him—fifteen years it turned out. Tim thought him quite handsome, as he accepted the drink. The music, flashing lights and movement of people around them weren't enough to mask the frisson between them.

Jack was a gentleman. He didn't, as so many had before, just expect a hook-up. He believed in true love. He even said he'd never really been in love until he fell in love with Tim. When Tim told Rachael this, and she sort of scoffed, said that seemed unlikely for someone who was nearly forty. But Tim knew it to be true, it had to be.

Jack hadn't had a loving childhood. Tim and Rachael's parents weren't particularly affectionate, but Jack's parents were down-right cold. Jack told Tim about their snobbery, their refusal to acknowledge that he was gay, the pressure they put on him to meet their expectations. How, as a result of all this, relationships had always been hard for him.

"But not with you. You're an old soul," he would tell Tim. "You match me."

So Tim strove to match him, always.

Looking back the abuse was an accumulation of little things. Incidents Tim had found a way to excuse for one reason or another. Jack had a high-pressure job, he was often tired after a long day, grumpy, put out by people on the underground or terrible traffic if he'd been driving. It was to be expected. Certainly, some things had seemed a bit unreasonable, like when Jack said he'd wanted to be alone and then snapped at Tim when he came downstairs an hour later, annoyed that he hadn't 'thought to bring him a cup of tea', but Tim tried not to dwell on those things.

There was the time when Rachael came for dinner, a dinner Jack had insisted on cooking so the siblings could chat, and after she'd left he'd been weird. Cold and distant, obviously upset. "You didn't try to include me in your conversation. How would you have felt if I'd had a co-worker around and all we'd done is talk about work?" Tim didn't really think he could argue with that one, had apologised and promised to do better next time.

"You'll know better for next time" was a refrain Jack often said — when Tim hadn't cleaned something to Jack's standards, or not put something away how Jack liked it. Tim would apologise, always, saying he was trying, he hadn't meant to upset Jack.

Tim tried, he really did. And he thought things were getting better after a while. When Tim paid attention, in the ways Jack reminded him to, things were okay. Jack wouldn't get irritated quite so often, and Tim got used to the fluttering in his chest.

And then the day came. There was a distance between them, and Tim was tired. He'd snapped at Jack, told him it was too hard, too much to keep loving him when Jack expected so much. Tim hadn't meant that things should end, he'd just wanted them to be different. He'd wanted to talk, to get back the easy understanding they'd seemed to have the first year they were together, to be the old soul that was Jack's match.

Jack's face had crumpled. He said Tim was right. He said he still loved Tim but just wasn't 'in love with him'. He didn't want to hold Tim back, keep him from happiness — and then Jack placed the ring, one of two they'd picked out together, the matching one on Tim's own hand, on the table between them.

Tim hadn't known what to do, what to say. He hadn't slept properly for days, fearful that he was the one who had fallen out of love, but at that moment, as Jack confirmed his greatest fears, Tim knew without a doubt that he did love this man.

He was numb, as he packed what he could into a few boxes and bags, loading up a neighbourhood street car. He was surprised at how little was his, how easy it was to remove himself from what had always been Jack's home, actually. Jack tried to help, told him he could take his time, get a van to move his stuff.

"I hate to see you so hurt, but I just want you to be happy."

"I was happy," Tim said, longing for Jack to say it was all a mistake, say he was willing to do the work, to make things fit again. But Jack just hung his head.

Tim removed clothes, a few design books, a jumper of Jack's that smelled of him, and drove back to his flat. He numbly brought the boxes up, dumping them in the near-empty closet of the flat's bedroom, a room he'd not used in years. Then he crawled onto the sofa, curled up into a ball, and tried to stop feeling anything.

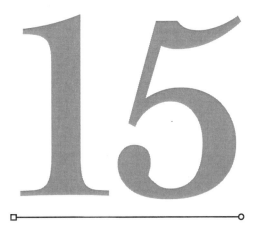

C helle doesn't have a lot of memories of her dad, but the few she does have she treasures. He was balding but kept his head shaved, so people couldn't tell, and a beard, which he kept neatly trimmed. He had a tattoo on his forearm of two entwined roses, which he told her was for her and her mum. He smelled of a strong aftershave, and he always wore white t-shirts and jeans. He could fix almost anything that went wrong in the house. But mostly what she remembers is how safe and warm and loved she felt when he was there.

He always asked Chelle how her day had been, wrapping her up in the nicest hugs. She'd breath him in, feeling her whole body relax in his big biceps. She marvelled at how large his hands were compared to hers, how tall he was, like her own personal, gentle giant. He would nibble her toes, play tickle monster with her, and then ruffle her hair and call her his little pixie.

Chelle hated being alone with her mum, hated the way she yelled and threw things, usually breakable items like ceramic mugs or dinner plates. His presence seemed to calm her down some, or at least prevented her from aiming those items at Chelle.

Most nights, after Chelle had gone up to bed, there would be a fight. It was always the same. Mum would have been drinking all afternoon, she'd be in a mood, start slagging him off. He would shout at her to calm down, probably take away her whisky or vodka or whatever she was chucking back like water. Then she'd either begin to cry, collapsing in a sobbing mess in his arms, or she would attack. Despite his size, her mother was always the one with the upper hand. The booze numbed her and her weapons were projectiles, one of Chelle's toys or an empty bottle of vodka thrown from across the room.

Despite the yelling, Chelle always managed to fall asleep, knowing it would blow over and in the morning her mum would be passed out on the sofa. Her dad would wake her up, tell her to get dressed. He'd bring her a bowl of cereal and say not to disturb her mum, that she'd had a rough night and needed to rest because she wasn't feeling well.

The night he left, Chelle remembers his large, strong frame silhouetted in the light from the hall as he stood in her doorway. She could smell his aftershave as he came close, kneeling next to her bed and resting his head on her pillow. He popped a little soft toy, a bunny, up over the bed and danced it towards her, making it nuzzle her face. She'd giggled, taking it from him as he ruffled her hair and stood up. He knelt over her and kissed her head, told her she would always be his little pixie. And then her memory goes soft around the edges. Chelle's never quite sure, when she thinks about it, if she did see a gash on his cheek or if she imagined it. She just knew the bunny, a soft blue colour, had a tiny spot of red on it, and she forever kept it hidden from her mum.

It took her several days to realise he wasn't coming back. Her mother wouldn't talk about it, and while she was drinking less, it was only because she no longer had access to his credit cards.

It didn't take long for them to get kicked out of where they were. By the time Chelle was eight they had bounced to three different council flats, finally settled into the one her mother would eventually die in.

Chelle hated it there, the stink of it, the way laundry piled up, that her mum smoked and drank and sat on the couch watching telly all day, getting bigger and bigger. It was Hell on earth, as far as she was concerned.

At eighteen she got out as quickly as she could, moving in with two girlfriends. They had a great little flat, three bedroom, one bath, a combined kitchen and dining room. It had been amazing, living away from her mother. Chelle worked at a salon part-time, doing nails, and as a bar girl on the weekends. Tips were good, and the clientele was pretty nice to her.

She had a few boyfriends too. Nothing especially serious. Just fun and easy.

Her life then had seemed so perfect, which was why finding out she was pregnant felt like the worst possible thing that could happen to her.

Her mum had only been seventeen when she'd had Chelle. There had been another baby before that, a miscarriage. There were three more miscarriages later. Chelle was 'the one that took' her mum used to say, but Chelle knew better. She hadn't been wanted, and she'd known it from the moment her dad had walked out. She'd known because her mum had made a point of telling her again and again, "What good is a kid if they don't make the father stick around?"

Chelle's mum made sure Chelle knew she was an insurance policy that hadn't paid off.

Chelle had gone to the clinic alone, and hated herself the entire time. The staff were so kind, though. They told her it was a common procedure and not one she should worry about. They told her there were counsellors on staff if she wanted to talk. They explained that this was her choice and would always be her choice.

She never regretted it, not once, and she also never told anyone—until she was in the pub with Darcy and the alcohol in her system, combined with the anonymity of talking to a near stranger, opened it all up. Darcy, nodding, said so calmly, "You know, none of this—your dad leaving and your mum being so abusive—is your fault, right? It never was."

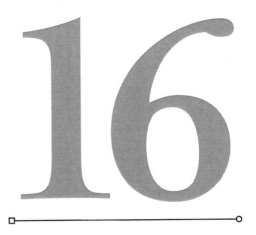

For the first year she lived there, when people asked Darcy why she came to London, she gave vague answers along the lines of it being a great place to explore, or because that's where she'd been accepted to study psychology, or most commonly "Why not?" If she were honest, though, Darcy would say it was because she was running away.

Not that 'why not' wasn't a factor, of course. If you were going to run away, why not run away to one of the world's biggest and most cultured cities?

It hadn't taken her long to realise that a person couldn't run away from their own silly self. Even though she saw it as a fresh start, and meeting and moving in with Felicity and Franklin had seemed like a way to start a new circle of friends, she was still Darcy from Calgary.

She'd decided that love was to blame. Such an unknowable emotion, if it could be called an emotion at all. A strange sensation that lives in the chest and stomach. A sense of longing perhaps, or a joyous rush of butterflies. Apparently spontaneous but also a lot of hard work, sometimes unconditional and, in Darcy's experience, rarely rational. She'd had a tight circle of friends back in Canada. They were all quite involved in theatre and perhaps their inclination towards all things dramatic contributed to what happened. There were five of them that counted as her core group and of the five, Percy was her best friend. They'd known one another since junior high and spent so much time together that people thought they were either dating or siblings—although the sibling thing was a bit of a stretch. Darcy's mum was half Chinese and her father, half Cree. Darcy had fair skin, high cheekbones, blue-black hair and dark eyes. Percy, however, was of European stock. He had soft, light brown hair, a face full of freckles and blue eyes.

When they entered High School, the one class they shared was Drama, and it was here Percy and Darcy met the other three who would make up what they dubbed 'the gang of rogues': Tall, trans Muriel, token hetero/white guy Stewart and throwing shade Frank, short for Francine.

Frank was the most morose of the bunch, with an air of mystery about her and a heavy dose of angst. Her inner arms, which she made no effort to cover up, showed purple and pink scars crisscrossed from her wrist to her elbow. She wore dark Cleopatra eyeliner, thick-soled platform shoes, corset tops and long velvet skirts of purple, black or deep blue.

Darcy admired Frank for her straight-forward approach to life. She made no excuses and refused to defend or pity anyone. When asked about her scars, Frank would say they were attention seeking 'bullshit' and that she was immature and dumb when she made them. She was confident in what she wore and how she wore it, completely unfazed by the stares or offhand insults of other students.

As a friend, Frank was the sort you wanted. She was excellent at listening and always gave sensible and sound advice.

And Frank was poly—as in amorous. She scorned what she described as the flawed system of monogamy and encouraged 'free love'—although she would have (and actually had) punched anyone who used such a hippie term.

Darcy and Frank began to date over the summer, just before grade twelve. To the group of friends, it had seemed a little odd. Frank usually kept her relationships incredibly informal. She wasn't part of a double act by choice, not circumstance, and the idea of her being in a couple was absurd. But there it was, Darcy had finally confessed her long-time crush and, much to her surprise, Frank reciprocated.

For a time things were blissfully happy for Darcy, but she learned how a single moment can change all that.

In the final semester, the senior students were busy preparing for the school's end of year production. Darcy and Frank were doing costume and set-design, and the two of them were in the tiny closet space where an abundance of wigs, moth-eaten costumes and boxes of props were stored. Darcy was meant to be going through the wigs to see which ones could be used and which ones would probably need to be chucked. Frank was supposed to be stitching up a hole in one of the dresses that had already been picked out for use. Instead, they were laying across a pile of clothes on the floor, snogging.

"Geez—you can get those stitches so close by hand. I don't know how you do it." Darcy pulled away, grinning at her girlfriend.

"It's about being patient. You can't think ahead to being finished. You just have to work on where you are," said Frank.

"Oh, grasshopper."

"Yes, oh grasshopper."

"But seriously, we need to get back to work." Darcy ran a finger down Frank's nose.

They picked themselves up, straightening their clothing and mussed hair, flirtatiously pawing at one another, as teenagers are wont to do. One of the grade ten students popped her head in the door, asking Darcy where she could find a mirror. Darcy rolled her eyes, told Frank she'd be right back, and went off to help out. She remembers this as being the last moment in school when she was really, truly happy.

Darcy was grinning as she left the tiny costume closet, trailing behind the younger girl. She must have passed Percy, but she didn't notice. She just remembers feeling elated at having made Frank laugh, and she was looking forward to further flirtation and silliness.

It took Darcy about ten minutes to locate a mirror and extract herself from the set-design team. She was talking as she opened the door to the prop and costume closet, although Darcy can't recall what she was saying. She just knew her mouth was open, mid-sentence, when she looked up and saw them. Percy was pressed against Frank, pushed against the hanging clothes. They pulled apart, and Frank smiled and said, "Uh oh."

Darcy looked at her best friend and then at her supposed girlfriend. They had talked about the poly thing, but Frank said part of the deal was full disclosure, and this was a total surprise. But what was more of a surprise was what Darcy felt at that moment — because she wasn't jealous of Percy kissing Frank, she was jealous of Frank kissing Percy. She had no idea what to do or say and so she'd just turned around and walked out.

Everything went funny after that. Frank and Percy stopped keeping their interest in one another a secret and Darcy extracted herself from the gang of rogues, despite Stewart and Muriel's efforts to remain friends. When one of the school counsellors approached Darcy with the prospect of a scholarship to attend King's College in London she thought 'Why not?'

Gian was at work when the call came about Antonio. They told him he needed to come down to the police station, but they didn't explain why. They just said it was about his son. He asked them not to call Bella. She was sensitive. Anything they had to tell him would need to be tempered before it reached her.

Gian always wanted a boy, a son to carry on the family name. He was proud when Ofelia was born, but nothing could match his joy when, a year later, Antonio came into the world. He did his best, he thought, to teach the boy how to be a man. Gian often wondered when things went wrong. As a teenager his son was disrespectful, prone to strange outbursts and running away. He would go out with his friends and not return for days, worrying Bella.

At first, it was merely a frustration, but one day when Antonio sneaked back into the house in the middle of the night, Gian confronted him. He demanded to know where he'd been, with whom, and what he'd been doing. Money had been going missing, and bits of Bella's jewellery. As if the boy knew how much it would hurt his father, Antonio pulled up the sleeve of the stained hoodie he wore, showing off the track marks with a smirk on his face. Gian told Antonio to leave and not come back until he'd gotten himself cleaned up. He had no time for junkies.

Bella was angry with Gian when he told her about it the next morning. "He's just a boy."

"He's nineteen. He's hardly a child at all anymore."

"But we're his family, Gian. We should be there for him."

"This is what he needs. Tough love, they call it. It's the best thing for him. Tough love to teach him that he can't play around like this. If we don't give him tough love, he'll just walk all over us. He's a sneak."

Ofelia, who was nearly twenty-one and looked more and more like her mother every day, was sitting on the sofa listening to their exchange. He remembers that she got up and left right about then.

On the day the police called, Gian thought he was prepared for the worst. He imagined Antonio was going to be charged for stealing, or possession, thrown into jail for an unknown duration. Gian feared for what it would do to Bella, how the stress would break her heart, but resolved not to worry himself, that it was for Antonio's own good.

At the police station, Gian was greeted by a young constable. The man took him gently by the arm, as though he were a woman.

"What is this? I hear my low-life son has been found by the police. Hopefully, you'll put him on the right track." Gian wanted them to know he had no illusions about Antonio's nature, that he didn't condone such a life and approved entirely of disciplinary action.

Of course, it was too late for that. They had found his son, or at least what they believed to be his son's body. They needed him to identify Antonio, and the constable was the one assigned to take Gian to the morgue to do so.

Gian's legs buckled and the constable, still holding his arm, helped him to sit down. In his chest, it felt as though his heart had ripped in two, an impossibly painful sensation. He struggled to catch his breath as he told the constable that they couldn't be right. It hadn't been so very long since he'd seen Antonio last, only a few weeks, three at the most. Surely they were mistaken?

But no, there was no error. Gian saw his boy's body himself and could not deny that it was his child they had found.

Telling Bella had been the hardest thing Gian had ever done in his life. She wailed when he broke the news, falling to her knees on the sitting room floor. He'd never seen her so distraught as he tried to comfort her. She clawed at the cushions on the couch, pushing her face into a crocheted throw, great, heaving sobs wracking her body. Ofelia, who had been standing in the hallway, pushed past him and took her mother in her arms, shooting him a look full of daggers. It was a look she would give him again, several years later, when Bella lay dying in a hospital bed after suffering a heart attack in the night. On that day his heart experienced the same intense pain it had with Antonio, and he's never felt that either wound has healed.

Gian didn't expect to be so alone in his old age. He wants his wife by his side, his son coming to visit with grandkids in tow, and his daughter able to smile at him with pride, or even just a hint of love.

Lifting his tired frame from the chair, Gian walks across the room to a large wooden cabinet. It's cumbersome, out of place in the condensed format of the flat, but he's grateful for the familiarity of it in an otherwise unfamiliar place. It's one of the few things he was able to rescue from the sale of furniture from the family home

From one of the middle drawers, Gian pulls out a Toscano cigar. It hasn't kept well, the papery surface is cracked and flaking. It's decades old, acquired during the last family trip they took to Italy when Ofelia and Antonio were still children. Though Antonio was only a boy at the time, no more than ten, Gian let him try one of the cigars he bought. He instructed him carefully, showing him how to prepare it, to light it and how to take that first gentle puff. Antonio inhaled far too deeply. He wretched and threw up onto the road, just outside the shop where Gian had purchased the Toscanos.

Gian smiles, remembering how Ofelia laughed, her giggle delightful and bright on that sunny, hot day. Bella scolded Gian playfully before taking Antonio into her arms, wrapping him in a big hug. Over Bella's shoulder, through watering eyes, Antonio beamed at Gian. "I'll do better next time, dad. When I'm older, maybe."

Gian ruffled his son's hair and told him he had done just fine.

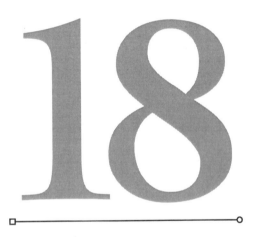

18

In the early hours of the morning, in a block of flats on the edge of Wimbledon, the residents of the second floor are all sleeping when the smell of smoke rouses one of them from a dream about her son getting married. She struggles out of her bed, tenderly setting her swollen foot, clad in an air cast, on the ground before grabbing her crutches and pulling on her dressing gown. She shuffle-hops into the sitting room to look out the window, but can't see any sign of smoke.

It isn't just a wood fire or something burning in the distance, though. The air is acrid, and so she suspects it's coming from somewhere in the building. She goes to the door, where the smell is strongest, and presses a hand against it. Finding it cold to the touch, she opens the door a crack, leaving on the chain. The hall is noticeably hazy. Moving as quickly as her ankle will allow, she picks up her phone and dials 999.

~ o ~

Namisha wakes with a start as her mobile phone begins to vibrate on the table next to her head. In his crib Malik twitches, making little noises in his sleep. She furrows her brow, rubbing her hands across her face and sitting up, grabbing the phone to silence it. A missed call with Hester's name glows on the screen. It's a little past four in the morning. As silently as she can, Namisha creeps from the bedroom, shutting the door quietly behind her. She's about the dial back when the phone begins to vibrate in her hand once more.

~ o ~

Chelle is curled up on her side in bed, Darren's arm wrapped around her, pulling her in tight. She tells him to turn off his alarm, that the noise is irritating, she's not working until late and wants a lie in. He squeezes her, yawns, and mumbles that it's not his alarm. Chelle realises she has to pee so she reluctantly peels herself from his arms and pads towards the bathroom. She pauses, noticing the smell of smoke. Rubbing her eyes she walks out into the sitting room, where the alarm is much louder. It takes her a moment, but she noticed the haze of smoke seeping in under the door.

~ o ~

Darcy flicks on her bedroom light and immediately covers her eyes with her arm to block out the harshness. Somewhere nearby an alarm is going off. It's persistent, loud and sharp. Pulling her duvet around her like a cape, she sits up, yawns and shakes her head. She can hear yelling coming from somewhere too, and her eyes are burning. She fumbles to grab her phone, to check the time, when Franklin bursts into the room.

~ o ~

Tim startles awake, his neck stiff from sleeping on the couch. Someone is hammering on his door and for a moment he thinks of the intruder, the look on Hester's face as she lay crumpled on the floor, the trip to the hospital. He feels like he's still dreaming, as the sound of an alarm pushes through the fog created by the sleeping pill he took. But then a familiar voice says his name, distinctively, and there's more pounding on the door. Chelle, he thinks. And then another voice, and a word, which makes the alarm and the strange haze he's noticing in the flat make sense.

"Fire!"

~ o ~

The morning dawns grey and cold in London, the sky overcast, a solid block of white cloud with no discernible texture. A crowd of people gathers on the pavement opposite the flats, a mix of residents, bystanders and emergency crews. A thick column of smoke rises up from the other side of the building, over the edge of the roof line. Several fire trucks block the road, as police re-direct traffic. A crackling roar can be heard over the din of shouting, engines, and sirens.

Someone is doing a headcount. The residents from the second floor stand in a group, taking comfort in being surrounded by familiar faces. They share their accounts of waking up, realising what was happening. It's one of the three youngest of them, an androgynous woman, who first notices that the count is wrong. There are only nine of them—there should be ten.

~ o ~

Gian is enjoying a lovely dream. He sits on a beach, the sound of the ocean mingles with the laughter of children. The air is briny and refreshing. Bella lies next to him, stretched out on her stomach, her back turning a lovely brown in the hot sun. Ofelia and Antonio play in the surf, running up and down and kicking sand at each other. Somewhere, off in the distance, someone is having a fire. Looking down the beach, Gian sees a large pile of detritus, old bits of driftwood and long, dried palm fronds. He realises the fire is actually much closer than he first thought and tries to tell Bella, but when Gian opens his mouth, he can't get enough air to speak.

He opens his eyes to darkness and sits up, the smell of smoke sharp and very real, not a dream at all. Gian waits for his vision to adjust but it doesn't. The bedroom is full of smoke—choking, thick smoke that burns his eyes. He tries to turn over, to lift himself from the bed. His lungs are like bricks in his chest. He's dizzy, disoriented, as he rolls to the edge of the old wooden bed. A coughing fit overtakes him as he falls to the floor. He has to get to the window, to get fresh air. He pulls the vest top he sleeps in over his nose and mouth, his eyes watering, barely able to stay open, and tries crawling across the floor. He hears the crackling of flames but doesn't know which direction it's coming from.

Rolling onto his back, Gian allows himself to cough again. Still holding the vest to his mouth and nose, he lifts his head to look up at the window and gauge if he could, in fact, reach it. Unable to breathe, Gian simply shuts his eyes.

In a moment he's dreaming again, back on the beach once more. It's dark now, night has fallen. The bonfire is still there, a bright flickering pile on the beach, the flames reaching up to touch the deep blue sky. Silhouetted against it are the forms of his children, their arms raised, toes pointed, as they dance on the sand.

EPILOGUE

◻————————————○

Namisha adores their new home. It's just right—a lovely ground floor Georgian flat with three bedrooms, a dining area and even a tiny bit of garden—only a short tube ride to her work, where she now has full-time hours. The proximity to her parent's home is more comforting than she could have imagined just a few short months ago.

Calling them after the fire had been incredibly difficult, but Hester insisted Namisha do it. "They're your parents. As a mother, I know I would want to know you were safe. Even if you've not been in touch for a long time, even if it's a challenge. And besides, you want to call, don't you?"

Of course, Namisha had to explain everything to Hester, so she understood that it was her father who chose not to have Namisha in his life, not the other way around. But Hester, wonderful, sweet Hester, knew better. "But it's not about your father, is it? It's your mum you miss."

It was hard at first, but better now that her mum knows she is safe and has met Malik. Things are still shaky with her father, but the flat—one of his many properties—is proof of something. It was her mother, largely, who convinced him to arrange for Namisha, Hester and Malik to live there, but Namisha knows he wouldn't have done it if he hadn't wanted to.

It's only been a few weeks since the three of them moved in, but there is already routine to their days. Namisha gets up, tends to Malik's breakfast and morning bath, and then passes him off to Hester so she can shower and dress for work. Her mother comes by most days, she and Hester competing to spoil Malik the most, their friendship blossoming. They see Namisha off, tell her to have a good day, and that they'll see her in the evening.

Namisha enjoys her work, the satisfaction and sense of accomplishment it gives her. She's started to make a few friends around the office, and they often lunch together or take walks along the Thames.

But by far, the best part of Namisha's day is when she comes home. She knows there will be a meal ready, and stories from both Hester and her mother, and she does look forward to this. But the best moment is as she walks up the street, and she can first see Malik in the window. He beams this huge smile at her, jumps down and a moment later, just as Namisha reaches the front walk, Hester will open the front door, and he'll come flying towards her. She catches her bundle of joy and excitement, wrapping him up in the biggest hug possible.

~ o ~

Chelle stands in the flat, so much like their old one but on the ground floor and in the other building unit. It's newly furnished, thanks to the insurance they had and a grant from a charity. Most of the damage was done not by the flames, which didn't spread far, but by smoke and the water used to put it all out. They couldn't keep anything but now, nearly a month later, just in time for Christmas, their new place is beginning to feel like home.

Chelle stands in the middle of the flat, alone. Darren has just popped down to the bins with a wad of plastic the new sofa came in. Despite the new space, despite everything that's happened, it doesn't feel like a fresh start. Her life is a constant series of unpreventable events which she has no say in.

After the fire, she went right back on the pill. She wasn't going to get pregnant with no home to raise a child in and now Chelle can't help feeling a sense of relief. She doesn't know what she wants besides knowing that this, right now, isn't it.

Sitting on the couch, which smells of sawdust and plastic, she runs her hands over the solid cushions. Her mother's voice is always there, like a song stuck in her head. She squeezes her eyes shut.

"You're dead. You're dead, and I don't have to listen to you," she says aloud, surprising herself.

"Who are you talking to?" Darren's says from behind her. She turns, startled, as she hadn't heard him come in. He closes the door, a worried expression on his face. "You okay, baby?"

"Yeah. Yes. Yes, I'm all right," she says, patting the cushion next to her. He sits down, taking her hands into his, looking her steadily in the eye. "I love you, Chelle."

"I love you too." She kisses him, softly and then a thought strikes her. She pulls away, raises an eyebrow and says, "Do you want to get married?"

~ o ~

The smell of bacon wafts into the spare room. Tim is lying under a pile of blankets. He knows he should stop thinking of it as 'spare' and start thinking of it as his, given that he's been here nearly a month, but he hasn't necessarily decided to stay. Rachael and her roommate are more than happy for him to use the space, of course. They insist he takes all the time he needs.

"And how much time you need isn't easily determined." Rachael reminds him, often.

He's beginning to realise his heart is more buoyant than he thought. The bruised quality is nearly gone. He even signed up on a dating app, tentatively putting himself out there again. Yesterday he was answering questions on the app, to help 'refine his searches', when the question 'Are you currently in love with someone?' popped up on the screen. He tapped 'No' without hesitation. It was only afterwards that Tim paused to consider this fact, to feel a release from hope, and a genuine sense of freedom to not love someone who had never loved him.

Tim's also joined an online forum for survivors of abuse. They often share how easy it is to fall into patterns of self-berating. It's why he's not dating just yet, only looking. He knows he isn't to blame for anything Jack did, but he doesn't always believe it. There are the memories he thinks of as good, moments when he and Jack had fun, or things were easy. It wasn't all bad, but it never is. That's the trick of it, the thing that Tim realises made it impossible for him to see the accumulation of problems—it was good enough just often enough.

Rachael's little points of wisdom, for which she takes no credit—claiming she's just being 'Buddhisty'—help prevent him from beating himself up too much.

"It wasn't your job to make him happy. It's never our job to make anyone else happy. That's something we get to own," she reminds him. "You just spend some time making yourself happy and see how that goes."

And Tim is happy, genuinely, in a way he hasn't been for a long time.

~ o ~

"I'm glad you're not alone," Jacob says, looking around the dining room. Hester smiles, not at his approval of her new living arrangement, but to try and ease his tension. He's only just arrived, and he seems apprehensive, nervous almost. Malik is on a walk with his grandmother, giving Jacob and Hester time and space.

"You said you had something you wanted to speak to me about?" Hester gestures to a chair, in an attempt to get him to sit down, but Jacob doesn't notice. He's pacing, which seems particularly intense in the small space, which forces him to pivot every four steps.

"Yes, I um..." He closes his eyes and takes a deep breath. "I have someone to introduce to you."

"Oh?"

"He's, I mean, I'll..." Jacob disappears through the doorway to the hall that leads to the front door. Hester listens to the click of the catch. She drums her fingers on the wooden table top.

A moment later the door clicks, and there is the low murmur of male voices. Jacob strides back into the room. He is followed by another young man, a man with a closely trimmed beard and short afro, large dark, umber eyes and a smile of such warmth Hester immediately stands and opens her arms to him. He strides into them and in her ear says, "It's so good to finally meet you."

For a moment she is entirely lost for words, as Hester hugs the man she knows is Adam, the elusive 'roommate' in Edinburgh. But only for a moment of course—as she pulls away she is a flurry of questions, as to why he is there and what happened and how they are back together. Her son is slightly shame-faced as Adam explains how Jacob's refusal to come out to Hester put a strain on their relationship but now, with everything in the open, they have patched things up. Hester is delighted at this turn of events and tells them so, but then remarks that Jacob is still pacing. "Is there something else?"

"There is," Jacob says, looking sideways at Adam, who reaches out and takes his hand. "I found my father."

~ o ~

Darcy lets go of Felicity and turns to Franklin, pulling him in for a hug. "I'm gonna miss you," he mumbles into the thick wool of her jumper.

"I'll miss you too. Seriously, though, I'm only going to be gone for a month. Besides, it's Christmas. You'll both be going home for most of it anyway."

"Still sucks." Franklin scuffs the ground with his foot. Felicity rolls her eyes and pushes his shoulder, but softly. "You are such a wimp."

Darcy grabs the handle of her luggage and looks toward the line for security. "I really should get going, or I'll miss my flight."

She gets into the line, turning to wave them off before they head in the direction of the underground.

There a clarity she's begun to experience ever since the fire. It wasn't that she'd felt like her life was in imminent danger, or that she might have actually died, but more that it changed what she'd always thought had mattered. Being right didn't matter so much. Being the martyr certainly felt entirely fruitless. Whatever she'd felt for Frank—admiration, envy, jealousy, even—had been about who she'd wanted to be. And any romantic ideas she'd been holding out for Percy seemed childish to her now.

When she told Felicity and Franklin about the whole palaver, they had been unified in a way that surprised her. Of course what had happened was awful, but what good did it do for Darcy to extract herself so entirely from a city she was fond of, a city where her family, whom she loved very much and who loved her very much, lived?

Her time away, in seclusion almost, out of a weird fear of encountering her old group of friends, is a self-flagellation she deeply regrets. Standing in the slow moving line for security, Darcy thinks of her parents and her grandparents, people who raised her, who love her unconditionally. For the last two years, they've been punished by her absence far more than Frank or Percy, both of whom Darcy finally blocked on Facebook on Felicity's recommendation. She couldn't argue with Felicity's logic that pain is plentiful enough without going looking for it, and Franklin's reminder that the best revenge is a life well-lived. She scoffed at them both, lightly teasing them for their saccharine sentiments, but inwardly she knows they're right. She imagines her heart as a little glowing ball of yellow light, happy to have friends like them

~ o ~

When Gian opens his eyes, he has to consider if he's still dreaming. He's in an unfamiliar room, which is bright, despite the gauzy curtains covering the windows and the weak winter sun. On a window ledge, in a part in the curtains, sits a vase full of flowers.

There's pain in his chest and throat and an odd tight sensation around his left arm. Gian tries moving it and finds he can't, he is weak, and it seems to be cemented down. He's unable to lift his head or swallow without it burning. In fact, Gian's entire body is alive with pain, pain aggravated by the rhythmic beeping of a machine somewhere just outside of his line of view. He has a vague recollection of nurses coming in, of having a tube pulled out of his throat at some point.

"You're awake."

He struggles to look in the direction of the voice that's just spoken but is quickly able to rest as Ofelia steps into his line of sight. She stands next to him, taking his right hand, which Gian realises he can move. She nods towards the vase of flowers in the window. "From the people in your old building."

He tries to speak, to tell her that he loves her, but his throat hurts far too much. Ofelia shakes her head. "Don't try to talk, dad."

She tells Gian he's been in a burn unit, in a semi-coma sort of state for several weeks, but that he's doing much better now. She pushes up a bit of hair that's fallen across his forehead and then rests her hand on his cheek. "You were lucky, dad. The doctor said you were probably almost entirely deaf because of a wax build up. Lucky that everyone on that floor was looking out for you, as you obviously didn't hear the fire alarm." Ofelia's voice breaks slightly, a crack in her familiar abrasive exterior. Gian keeps his eyes locked on her face, noting the way her eyes look so much like Bella's, and how she has his mouth and chin.

Ofelia looks towards the window, but her eyes are focused on something not in the room. She speaks slowly, maintaining her poise to hold back her emotions, "Seemed strange to me that they'd want to buy you flowers. You made it sound like they were a bunch of chavs and drug addicts."

She laughs, her eyes refocusing, returning to the room. Gian squeezes her hand, enjoying the warmth and softness of her fingers resting on his palm and wrist. "I can't imagine the old woman, Hester, is it? As a drug addict... She does go on, though."

Gian nods slightly, turning the corners of his mouth up into a weak smile. He squeezes Ofelia's hand again, and she looks down, as if only just realising they are still touching. He is afraid, for a moment, that she will pull away, and a small sound escapes his raw throat. But then she places her other hand over his and squeezes back.

ABOUT THE AUTHOR

Kaitlyn (AKA 'Kait') is a Canadian-born Creative Polymath and Buddhist. She lived in the UK for six years where she gained citizenship and a strange amalgamated Canadian-English accent. She also drinks a lot of tea. This probably didn't qualify her to write a book full of British characters and set in London, but she doesn't care, she wrote it anyway.

She can't say where in the world she lives at the moment but 'home' is with her wife, Gretchen, and fur-child, Delirium, who may be a cat but may *also* be an Ewok/lemur/squirrel/owl/monkey-cross.

In addition to writing books, Kait keeps a blog, runs a podcast, does graphic design and makes art.

MORE FROM KAIT

The official website of All of the Things, including her art and design portfolios and her blog.
www.KaitlynSCHatch.com

Everything is Workable: A podcast that examines how every experience, every situation, every moment is an opportunity to work with our mind.
everythingisworkable.podbean.com

Wise at Any Age: A handbook for cultivating wisdom, first published in 2013.
Available through her website and on lulu.com

Lets kill the myth of the starving artist together!

Visit Kait's website to find out how you can contribute to the production of *Everything is Workable*, the publication of more books, and the creation of more art.